EVERYGNOME'S GUIDE TO PARATECHNOLOGY

YOUR ESSENTIAL RESOURCE FOR SURVIVING
EXPLOSIONS, AVOIDING MUSTACHE TANGLES,
MOVING BEYOND BASIC CLOCKWORK DEVICES,
AND ADVANCING AS A MASTER OF
METAMAGICAL PURSUITS

JOSEPH J. BAILEY

CONTENTS

PREFACE

The EA'AE books are guides one might happen upon within the larger multi-verse created in the *Chronicles of the Fists, Orc PI,* and *Spellslinger Chronicles* trilogies... fantasy books giving farcical (or practical) advice for professions that don't exist (even if we may want for them to... or not).

You have been warned.

EVERYGNOME'S GUIDE TO PARATECHNOLOGY

Everygnome's Guide to Paratechnology

Your Essential Resource to Surviving Explosions, Avoiding Mustache Tangles, Moving Beyond Basic Clockwork Devices, and Advancing as a Master of Metamagical Pursuits

Joseph J Bailey

EVERYGNOME'S GUIDE TO PARATECHNOLOGY

Your Essential Resource for Surviving Explosions, Avoiding Mustache Tangles, Moving Beyond Basic Clockwork Devices, and Advancing as a Master of Metamagical Pursuits[1]

Translated from the Gnomish by
Joseph J. Bailey[2]
TINKER

Notes to self (and others):

1. *Or a brave attempt thereon.*
2. *As originally cataloged by the illustrious Spreesprocket Goldpulley.*

AUTHOR'S NOTE

This brief, somewhat esoteric treatise is intended for Gnomes who aspire to create their heart's desires without blowing themselves or anyone else up.

If your heart has no desires, or you wish to be blown up, this book is not for you.

GNOME'S NOTE

For those who are Paratechnologists, this tome will remain unencrypted and readily available.

For non-Paratechnologists, including most Dwarves seeking to become Paratechnologists, this treatise will appear to be a concise, perhaps overwritten, thesis on the many wondrous uses of snail slime for health and self-improvement.[1]

Notes to self (and others):

1. I do offer my sincerest apologies to all snails both in advance and hereafter.

To those who imagine,
but, more importantly, to those who aspire.

FROM FLASHWHISTLE BOOMBLASTER

Paratechnology is hazardous and not at all safe. Your choices only generally make it more so.

Before attempting any Paratechnological activities, be sure to don safety goggles, gloves, and an adamantium overcoat, all decidedly and absolutely reinforced.

Additional precautions are strongly advised.

- Flashwhistle Boomblaster
Post-Technological Metamagician to the Nth Degree, Squared

EVERYTHING YOU NEED TO KNOW ABOUT PARATECHNOLOGY IN THREE1 PARAGRAPHS OR LESS

Despite what some may claim, Paratechnology is not the mere juxtaposition of perceived opposites, the blending of magic and technology in their myriad forms and expressions, the imbuing of mechanical objects with eldritch enchantment, or even the grand thread tying together systems within and outside the limits of understanding.

Paratechnology is the synthesizing of impossibles, the merging of the absurd, the transcending of the mundane, and the joining of the unimagined!

Paratechnology is the very bridge between the possible and the inconceivable.[2]

Get building![3]

Notes to self (and others):

1. *Or four. Paratechnology is as flexible as it is wondrous.*
2. *For more somewhat related reference information, please see the diverse glossary of terms included at the end of this guide.*
3. *Where's my toolbox?*

DO I HAVE WHAT IT TAKES?

Indubitably!

Although historically a high Gnomish Art requiring utmost technical skill and unrivaled magical precision, Paratechnology is now open to any and all comers.[1]

We welcome any of sound, or at least echoing, mind, able, or partially functional, body[2], and boisterous spirit, the more zest the better, to partake of our grand tradition.

If you think[3], breathe[2], have a pulse[2], and are able to communicate at least through coarse grunts or vague gestures, consider a career in Paratechnology![4]

Your local Gnomes will take care of the rest![5]

The true beauty of Paratechnology is that almost anyone can learn to actively shape reality.[6]

I would, however, recommend growing facial hair before you start.[8]

Notes to self (and others):

1. *Significant attrition within the Gnomish community through the practice and rarefication of Paratechnology to its current highly refined state has encouraged the most welcome inclusion of many non-Gnomes into the halls of Paratechnological wonder.*
2. *Or rough equivalent thereof.*
3. *Or can convince others that you can.*
4. *Also recommended is an almost complete disregard for your health, well-being, and safety. Understanding relatives and relations who are comfortable with your possible loss, disappearance, and/or expiry is advised.*
5. *Not that you will necessarily enjoy much rest but, rest assured, when you do, it might just be peaceful.*
6. *For some non-Paratechnologists, this might be a cause for some concern.*[7]
7. *Being compassionate, wise, and far-seeing, we Paratechnologists also have concerns for causes.*
8. *If you cannot grow facial hair, I suggest donning a disguise or having a mustache transplant, infusion, or restructuring to begin your career. Once you reach a certain level of success, acceptance, and maturity, then you* may *outgrow the need for facial hair... but that is unlikely.*

WHY BE A PARATECHNOLOGIST?

Do you like fun?
   Who doesn't?

Do you appreciate excitement?
   I really hope so.

Do you get a thrill from new discoveries?
   Getting a thrill from old discoveries counts as well.

Do you remain in the room when someone opens a science, magic, or mathematics textbook?
   Being tied down, chained, mind controlled, drugged, or rooted in place through sorcerous compulsion does not count.

Do you have impeccable fashion sense?
   Absolutely critical.

. . .

Do you like objects that are shiny?
    If not, you are probably dull.

Do you like to shape the future?
    Shaping dough, clay, putty, and the like counts as well.[1]

Do you appreciate the beauty in great balls of fire engulfing your life's work?
    Who doesn't like a fresh start?

If you said "yes" to all of the above[2], then the wondrous world of Paratechnology beckons!

I am a Paratechnologist.

There is no finer calling.[3]

Why aren't there more of us?[4]

Notes to self (and others):

1. *Although a willingness to shape ideals is preferable.*
2. *Saying "yes" to any of the above really suffices. Our standards as Paratechnologists are rather forgiving.*
3. *And my aural spectrum registers across the entire frequency range of sonic oscillation. I have yet to miss a call, especially to dinner.*
4. *Excepting the risks posed by a few minor workplace hazards—like dimensional tears and rifts, violent conflagrations, minor (and major)*

explosions, out-of-control automatons, antimagic and antimatter explosions, vengeful Luddites resistant to innovation, exponentially expanding self-replicating swarms of matter-consuming nanobots, overzealous competitors, losing your mind (both literally and figuratively), pertinent oversight boards, visitors, deliverymen, neighbors, and paper cuts... among others.

RULES TO LIVE BY

Paratechnology is about learning, experimenting, and progressing. The more mistakes you make, the more you will learn.

Expect to make many.[1]

The more you think you know, the less you actually do.

The less you do, the less you learn.

No one mind encompasses the totality of existence.[2]

No matter how grand a theory, no matter how elegant a solution, no matter how learned a theoretician, chances are they do not know it all... though they may act like it.

Approach each problem with humility and an open mind that you may learn.

Approach each problem earnestly that you may grow.

. . .

Expect to fall flat on your face often (usually accompanied by smoke, rushing air, bursts of small particulates, gouts of magical energies, walls of heat, and loud explosions).

Be intelligent in how you fall.[3]

Be even more intelligent in how you pick yourself back up.

Being careful may keep you safe, but it won't guarantee results.[4]

Being safe will, however, help ensure your continual persistence that you may reiterate the importance of being safe.[5]

Although doing nothing is fun, sometimes doing something is the best thing to do.[6]

Try not to die. At least not until you're ready to do so.[7]

Uncovering innovation is a bit like hunting for mushrooms. You don't have to know everything about mushrooms or about the area you're looking for mushrooms in, but some knowledge helps.[8] And more knowledge is often, but not always, better.[10]

Notes to self (and others):

1. _Present company included._
2. _Especially those of your fellow technologists._
3. _With my protuberant nose this is of utmost consideration._
4. _Nor will you have as much fun._
5. _For those who care to listen._
6. _Say that three times fast._
7. _Then feel free._
8. _You may also need to be prepared to dig through quite a bit of manure in your search._[9]

9. *Assumed is that you know what types of mushrooms you are after. Finding the right mushrooms is essential. If you select the wrong mushrooms (or ideas), then your adventure of discovery may be of an altogether different sort.*
10. *Unless you're a know-it-all. Then less is more.*

YOUR EDUMACATION

Do you wish to excel at Paratechnology?

Then you must swim through the fields of metamagics, applied, theoretical, and notional physics, suprachemistry, future history, developmental and cognitive parapsychology, antientropics, idealized engineering, archmathematics, extrabiology, synthetic intelligence, ultracosmology, schema, yarn spinning, and multimodal computational panlogic, among many others, as easily as a fish darts through clear, untroubled waters.

No area of intellectual endeavor should be neglected, nor should your quest for deeper understanding ever stop—for with knowledge's end, so follows innovation's.

Also, you must be able to tie your shoes.
Above all else, this is critical.[1]

Notes to self (and others):

1. *The last thing you need as a Paratechnologist is to fall flat on your face.*[2]
2. *Your projects will do that for you.*[3]
3. *Frequently.*

YOU IN THE EYES OF FELLOW SCHOLARS, TECHNOLOGISTS, AND MAGICIANS

Hopefully you are not in anyone's eyes unless asked. Invading others' personal space without permission can be dangerous and outside ethical norms.

Also, it might hurt.

That said, you are a hybrid.

You take the best of many disciplines and make them your own.[1]

As an amalgam, you may not be welcome, understood, or fully appreciated by practitioners of other advanced specialties ranging from magic to medicine.

Your multidisciplinary expertise may, at times, be viewed as a challenge or threat to more traditional Crafts.

Their loss is your gain!

Their ignorance, reticence, and lack of foresight only reflect the holes in their knowledge, the failings and shortcomings of their worldviews.

Fill those gaps with your expertise![2]

Mind the nooks and crannies that you may stuff with inventive exuberance!

Overwhelm their uncertainty with positive contributions to their fields!

Only through improvements upon old ideas will new ones be accepted.

Notes to self (and others):

1. *You may not always take the absolute best, but you certainly take from other disciplines!*
2. *Preferably with something non-explosive. Let their changes in understanding represent the true explosions.*

TWO WRONGS OFTEN MAKE A RIGHT

Except when they don't.[1]

There is a certain beauty and symmetry to be found in the truly awful, the stupendously bad, and the downright impossible.

Bringing together and then overcoming the failed and misguided attempts of others only magnifies your success and the validity of your work.

Do not confine yourself to the simple, the easily attained, the elegant, the trite, the beautiful, the desired, or the desirable.

These are realms for common inventors.

That you can bring novelty and wonder to the insignificant, the horrid, and the rejected is a badge of honor among Paratechnologists![3]

Wear your badge proudly!

Aspire to be yourself and express your own ideals.

Make a path few are able (or willing) to follow.

. . .

Notes to self (and others):

1. *A rarity, I assure you.*[2]
2. *Sometimes they make a multiverse-shattering interdimensional rift. But I digress.*
3. *Badges are a welcome addition to any Paratechnologist's ensemble.*[4]
4. *Especially ostentatious ones.*

BRANCHES OF PARATECHNOLOGY

Generally speaking, there are several major areas of Paratechnological practice and study:

Tinkering – the traditional and historical root of Paratechnology. Before Gnomes ever succeeded in blending magic and machines, there were Gnomes tinkering with (and often breaking) everyday devices in their efforts to make them better, derive new uses from common things, create entirely novel items, and uncover undiscovered applications for their creations.[1]

Clockwork devices are one of the most common and widely recognized examples of this formative branch of Paratechnology. Today, even the simplest clockwork device may be imbued with enchantments and technologies far beyond the understanding or expectation of early Gnomish inventors.

Transmogrification – a slightly more refined form of tinkering that involves changing one type of object into another, often by blending the properties of two items together or adding novel, unexpected facilities to devices otherwise not so imbued.

Transmogrification is not limited simply to adding new capabilities to items or merging one object with another. Transmogrification also provides a means to personal transformation as well as the metamorphosis of one article into another.

Alchemical – Paratechnological alchemy revolves around understanding the higher chemistries of the macroverse's workings, and the changes that occur between various functions, states, manifestations, sets, fields of study, and frames of view. Just as physical laws govern natural phenomena and metamagical laws govern magical occurrences, alchemical laws govern the interactions between the two.

A Paratechnological alchemist must always have his head in the clouds and his feet on the ground.[2]

Suprachemistry – the study of how magical and nonmagical systems, compounds, elements, entities, and components interact, react, behave, change, and develop. Suprachemistry has historically focused on reactions and interactions on a microscopic scale. However, given the computational capabilities of Paratechnology systems and synthetic intelligences, macroscopic studies, representations, and creations are currently just as common.

Noetic – the broad, applied study of the mind, its capabilities, and extensions. The mind is a wondrous instrument and the Paratechnologist's most valuable tool. Extending its capabilities, making it more efficient and effective, and developing new faculties for Gnomish (and non-Gnomish) intelligences fall under the noetic sciences.

Understanding and heightening the mind are not the only focus of the noetic arts. Instead they are but the beginning. The creation and development of synthetic intelligence capable of abstraction orders of magnitude greater than an embodied intelligence represents an extension of the noetic arts. Abstracts and Constructs are but two of many such achievements. Bridging the artificial, or created, mind and the natural, or biologic, intelligence provides another vibrant area of study within the Gnomosphere.

Taken together, the noetic arts extend the realm of understanding at an ever-increasing rate, constantly opening new horizons of discovery while expanding the limits of the possible.

Parapsychology – the magical study of the mind, its features, moods, states, and manifestations. Parapsychology is the historical source of the noetic arts and remains an allied science.

In the present day, parapsychological research centers around mental understanding, particularly of novel species and modes of intellectual expression, while the noetic sciences focus more on the application of that understanding through creations such as synthetic intelligences like magical thinking machines.

Future history – the Paratechnological study of outcomes and possibilities. Far beyond mere statistical probability analysis, future historians map possible outcomes and likely events both within this universe and others.

Studies include the birth of alternate universes, event-solution path optimizations, the end of time and time after time, the beginning of the end, and the end of the beginning along with the beginning of the beginning and before the beginning.

Archmathematics – higher-order mathematics, modeling, and cognitive frameworks used in Paratechnological studies. Archmathematics provides the theoretical framework for studies in disciplines ranging from notional physics to metamagics and idealized engineering to future history.

When simple mathematics aren't enough, Paratechnologists go further by using archmathematics![3]

Antientropics – the study of creating energy and adding energy back to systems, devices, and entities.

Typically viewed as a subset of notional physics and metamagics, antientropics plays an important role in idealized engineering, creating and manipulating pocket dimensions, biomimetics, augmentation, and transmogrification.

Metamagics – traditionally understood as the bridging of diverse magical fields, or the study thereof, metamagics goes well past mere linkages between magical disciplines.

In a sense, Paratechnological metamagics is the study of magic in and of itself, its laws, and governing principles. Through metamagical study, Paratechnologists seek to uncover and understand the very nature of magic itself. From this deepening understanding, novel Paratechnological applications, theories, and ideas are ever-evolving.[4]

Notional physics – the foundational study of the higher (and lower) laws of the universe, the greater megacosm, and its assorted subsets. Notional physics includes both theoretical and applied branches along with many subsets.

Notional physics finds its expression and extension in various branches of

Paratechnological endeavor, including idealized engineering, alchemical studies, ultracosmology, suprachemistry, and metamagical research.

Notional physics studies include an array of topics ranging from examining dark and light magic and their influence on the fate of the macroverse, antientropic universal energy states and positive energy influx on the universal energy continuum, the creation, annihilation, and generation of matter and energy, the formation and expression of alternate dimensions, high-level string theory (i.e. how to tie shoe strings), the shape of the multiverse (and baked goods), and theories of magic, the universe, and everything.[5]

Augmentation – an extension of transmogrification focused on the permanent change of one's self or an object, generally with heightened capabilities. Augmentation often receives its inspiration from nature, taking forms and shapes, inherent talents and abilities, from other races, species, and phenomena and imbuing them in creative combinations.

Coupled with transmogrification, augmentation allows Paratechnologists to become beings of pure energy or thought, humanoid dragonids, robotic pan-human hybrids, computational machines, or any other representation within the Gnome's understanding and ability.

When being a Gnome is not enough, augmentation provides a readily available avenue to become whatever your heart desires.

Idealized engineering – the practical translation of Paratechnological ideas to actuality. Idealized engineering includes the application, study, and process of making the expression of Paratechnological ideas and technologies more efficient and effective. Idealized engineering also includes the study of improving technological understanding, application, refinement, and development. Simply put, idealized engineering is the creative application of Paratechnological principles.

How does a Paratechnologist bring an idea to life? Through idealized engineering!

Schema – the patterning, diagramming, representation, and planning of Paratechnological devices, theorems, strategies, and abstractions. Most closely related to idealized engineering, schema is often the first step (after having the notion) in bringing a conception to reality.

An idea is just an idea until the pen is put to page.[6] Paratechnologists skilled in schema are quite literally able to bring pictures to life.

After all, what's a clever toy without a nice representation?

Multimodal computational panlogic – the theory of structured and unstructured reasoning, rational and irrational decision-making, and generally making things up.[7]

Multimodal computational panlogic finds its particular expressions in the creation, modification, and improvement of various modes and representations of intelligence.

Extrabiology – the extension and expansion of biological systems, processes, and manifestations. This field includes both the alteration of extant life forms as well as the creation of novel ones.

Combined with biomimetics, transmogrification, and augmentation, the creation of almost any type of living being is possible.[8]

Give a Gnomish Paratechnologist free rein over evolution and one can only imagine what surprises are in store!

Yarn spinning – the fine art and noble tradition of Gnomish storytelling and tale tales. Yarn spinning is your first (and least damaging) line of defense when your audience's eyes start to glaze over.

Your work should speak for itself. However, greasing the wheels of innovation never hurts.

Biomimetics – the area of Paratechnological research that focuses on the understanding of biological functions, their governing principles, improvement, and alteration. Biomimetics provides the foundation for Gnomish medicine, cures and preventions for myriad diseases, and the elimination of genetic abnormalities.

Beyond basic health and quality of life, biomimetics provides a path to embodied immortality, boundless health and energy, strict control over the body's biochemical, physical and mental states, and regeneration, as well as personal health and growth.

There are, of course, many other branches of Paratechnological study, just as there are many more branches waiting to be uncovered.[9]

This, the imminent, is where you come in![10]

Your career represents the future of Paratechnology![11]

Notes to self (and others):

1. *Or just learning how to blow things up.*
2. *He must also always be simultaneously on the lookout for flying objects and tripping hazards.*
3. *Archmathematicians are easily identifiable and most frequently found scratching their heads.*
4. *For additional discussion on metamagics, see Mulogo's wonderful* Codependent Arising and Generation of Life, Magic, and the Real.
5. *For a thorough overview of notional physics theory, I highly recommend David Gnohm's* Wholeness and the Explicate Order.
6. *Or, more accurately, thought is put to action.*
7. *Gnomes are good at this.*
8. *Including those that are not (possible).*
9. *These branches can be convoluted, confusing, and esoteric. Many may need to be trimmed.*
10. *Be prepared to soar! Your only limits are those of your own imagination!*
11. *May it be as bright and shiny as my bald pate on a cloudless day after a thorough waxing.*

MAKING THE PERFECT LABORATORY

Is largely a concern of the past.[1]

With the nearly limitless computational, simulational, and existential capabilities of the Construct and its equivalents, determining the most likely outcomes of experiments is as simple as requesting, calling up and modeling the appropriate variables and desired outcomes.[2] Given the desired final properties of your creation, manifesting a representation of your ideal is even simpler.[3]

Of course, there will always be those for whom experiments should be a "hands-on" endeavor.

For those[4], I recommend a structurally reinforced chamber, region, or space capable of withstanding the most fearsome blasts, one impervious to the raging energies of the highest heavens, one sufficiently encapsulated and self-contained so as not to disturb the neighbors[5], and one capable of fully isolating and containing any extradimensional abnormalities (sentient or otherwise) that may manifest within your workspace.

Appropriate safety gear and multiple egress points are also advisable.[6]

Also, I would *not* advise keeping any items of sentimental, posited, or tangible value therein.[7]

Notes to self (and others):

1. *Though some always have concerns for the present.*
2. *For most conceivable scenarios. Since we often deal in the inconceivable, computation, simulation, and modeling along with the continued expansion of intelligence are freely employed in all areas of Paratechnological endeavor.*
3. *Assuming you would like a physical manifestation. If your creations are like mine, oftentimes this is undesirable.*
4. *Like myself!*
5. *Assuming any are brave enough to live next door or within a respectable blast radius.*
6. *Particularly when one disregards the considered recommendations of the Construct or its attendant Abstracts.*
7. *Unless of course you really do not want said item (like last year's mustache trimmer). Then feel free to leave it in the lab.*

YOUR LIBRARY

Is really unnecessary.

Every document, scroll, tome, or text you need, may need, think you need, or will ever need can be accessed directly through multiple dimensions, access parameters and interaction protocols via an Abstract or through the Construct.[1]

Documents that are not presently accessible are easily uploaded[2] once acquired, whereupon they will acquire levels of insight, instruction, and utility heretofore unimagined or anticipated by their original creators.[3,4]

If not presently available, the desired information can almost always be interpolated or extrapolated from extant data and computational resources.

Beyond traditional passive learning modalities, betterment options available through Paratechnology include the direct transfer of knowledge, skills, and experiences across various noospheres, modes of being, and realms of existence. Also accessible are simulational learning experiences in immersive environments of assorted mind and reality states, embodiment in alternative forms, settings, and capabilities, and direct exposure to alternate living experiences.[5]

Although finding, perusing, and savoring books is as noble as it is fun, directly interacting with a living, sentient representation of the knowledge therein is breathtaking.[6]

Having shelves of books, piles of scrolls, and stacks of reports artfully arranged in your study does, however, create a nice contemplative aesthetic and may impress your guests!

Notes to self (and others):

1. *Assuming you are wise enough to take advantage of the resources.*
2. *Directly to your mental substrate, the Construct, an Abstract, or the like.*
3. *This succinct treatise being one such minor example.*
4. *You will, however, have to be patient and wait for those documents not yet created to be uploaded… unless you wish to create them.*
5. *See* The Good Stuff: Select Mind-State Enhancements, Heuristics, Empowerments, Worldviews, Skill Sets, Traditions, & Knowledge Bases *for many practical examples.*
6. *To say the least.[7]*
7. *Especially for those of us who don't get out much.*

WHAT DOESN'T KILL YOU CAN ALSO MAIM, DESTROY, AND DISFIGURE

You don't want to be blown up.

You probably don't wish to be melted.

I would guess you would prefer not to be fused to a metallic, siliceous, mineral, or organic substrate.

Nor would you desire annihilation, negation, contagion, memory wipe, unexpected personality change, or extradimensional imprisonment.

You probably don't dream of being eaten, blasted, burned, atomized, phase changed, imploded, densified, reconstituted, or squashed.

When you were young I would hazard to guess that you did not aspire to grow up and be decimated, mutilated, aborted, ravaged, mangled, nuked, mutated, or spoliated.[1]

Have a bit of care.

Paratechnologists are not masochists.[2]

. . .

We understand (but often try to break, tweak, and recalibrate) the laws of cause and effect.

Recognize the dangers and hazards of your chosen profession.
   They are many.[6]
   You are not.[7]

What doesn't kill you may maim, destroy or disfigure; but a good idea may remedy all your problems and leave you better off than when you started.[8]
   In this case, what doesn't kill you may also make you cooler. Or, if you're really good, *shinier*.

Notes to self (and others):

1. *Unless of course these are all part of your plans. If so, then please carry on.*
2. *Paratechnologists are eccentric.[3]*
3. *And usually, but not always, Gnomish.[4]*
4. *Most frequently with elaborate facial hair.[5]*
5. *We are, however, hard at work to expand upon these limitations.*
6. *For a nonexhaustive but rather imaginative primer on other potential risks for practitioners of the arcane arts, see* Mulogo's Treatise on Wizardry.
7. *At least until you have perhaps undergone a thorough round of personal transfiguration and/or augmentation.*
8. *Particularly if said idea involves clever augmentation.*

BEING YOURSELF (OR NOT)

There are those who say the universe (or, for the more broad-minded, the macroverse) has a plan for them.[1]

I say, *have a plan for yourself.*

You are a Paratechnologist.
The possible is your plaything.
The impossible is your playground.

Whatever you wish to be, whatever you hope to become, you are able.
All that is required is a little hard work, the right application of knowledge, a bit of discovery, and not blowing yourself up.[3]

Notes to self (and others):

1. *As though the infinite unfolding of reality and collapse of probability into actuality were not enough on the multiverse's plate.[2]*
2. *Personally, I prefer a nice steaming pile of lightly seasoned rutabagas on my dishware.*
3. *Proper GPE, Gnomish Protective Equipment, is generally advised.*

MOVING BEYOND CLOCKWORK DEVICES

First and foremost, there is absolutely nothing wrong with a clockwork device, particularly one incorporating intelligent enchantments and imbued with flash and flourish.[1]

There is a proud legacy of clockwork devices in the Paratechnological tradition. In many ways, clockwork devices *are* the Paratechnological tradition.

However, clockwork devices, and the perception that most Paratechnological objects and creations are clockwork devices, holds back the advancement and spread of our grand Art.

Preconception and prejudice are the bane of the evolution of intellectual endeavor and anathema to our Art.

As astounding as clockwork devices are and have been, we cannot let past accomplishments interfere with future efforts.

While appreciating the past, we must ever move to the future.[2]

Notes to self (and others):

1. *In truth, clockwork devices have a decidedly wonderful character and*

style worth emulating and building upon… hence their persistence within the Art.

2. *Unless of course we are moving toward the dinner table.[3]*
3. *Particularly one with a wide assortment of root vegetables.[4]*
4. *Then Paratechnology can wait… or help. Your choice.*

HOW TO DEAL WITH PROFESSIONAL SETBACKS

Every failure is an opportunity.[1]

You merely have to have the courage to see them as such. Once apprehended, you must then muster the wherewithal to act.

With the right perspective, anything is possible.

With perspective comes the opportunity for change.

Do your colleagues mock your equations on the strong correlations between entropic development and expression in the macrocosmos, living beings' attempts to secure freedom to act through maintaining an optimal array of future histories, and the evolution and refinement of intelligence?[2]

Allow their skepticism to spur your research further!

Has your latest invention—a self-perpetuating non-holographic Omnicron capable of generating and sustaining immersive, non-virtual actualities—fallen on deaf ears?

Raise your voice in song and yodel the praises of your ideals![3]

. . .

Do your sponsors time your perpetual motion machine, constantly checking their pocket watches to see how long it will move and when it will stop?[5]

Build another!

Better yet, incorporate some unexpected surprises for them to enliven their study! Imagine their shock when your perpetual motion machine goes in reverse, crumbles apart and rebuilds, serves drinks, or shakes, trembles, and belches smoke at random, all the while chugging inexorably along.

Does your mentor doubt the efficacy of your sub-quantum mustache disentangler, sparkler, and body hirsuteness enhancer?

Give him a demonstration on his pocket fairy's whiskers![6]

Do your fellow researchers snicker at your latest FTP (faster than physics) communication protocol, taunting that a string and two tin cans is a more effective way to share data across cosmic dimensions and space-time?

Prove them wrong by whispering a secret in their ears before they even know they had that secret to tell!

With a bit of wit and humor, you can invoke the most powerful change of all, that of altering another's mind.[7]

Notes to self (and others):

1. *Most especially if you're opportunistic.*
2. *See Wissner-Gross and Freer's excellent primer entitled* Causal Entropic Forces *for introductory theory.*
3. *If you sing like me, however, this may hurt rather than help your cause.*[4]
4. *In that case, you may want to consider ear plugs... or murmuring.*
5. *Offer them basic theory along parallel lines while they natter about. For instance, conjure some light reading along the lines of Wilczek's* Quantum Time Crystals *to idle the time away while they wait.*

6. *Assuming said pocket fairy is in agreement. The last thing he or she needs is an even crotchetier pocket fairy!*

7. *Of course, there are many ways to change another's mind available to the Paratechnologist, but those generally are a bit more literal than figurative.*

WHEN YOUR APRON CATCHES FIRE

Be prepared.[1]

When your multispectrum acculenses catch your mustache on fire, you need a backup plan.[5]

When your volatile reagents volatilize your clothing, I suggest a spare set of garments.[6]

When your homunculus or familiar absconds with your favorite tool just as you are putting the final adjustments on your project, you need an alternate solution.[8]

When your floating can of frictionless oil spills on the floor and you fall flat on your face, you need a self-actuated occupational hazard emergency mop.[9]

· · ·

Personally, I recommend maintaining a legion of safety devices on hand for the highly unlikely (but quite too frequent) bouts of excitement that will befall you, your laboratory, and your related Paratechnological endeavors.

Although contingency spells are a must, particularly for those events dealing with personal safety, having sentient autonomous devices, objects, and intelligences that can react accordingly will further increase your chances of both success and survival. ARMED, NUMEN, EGAD, ENNIS, and SAVERS are especially helpful, germane, and desirous in this regard.[10]

Also, it's nice to have recording devices stationed strategically around workspaces and locales to catch reactions and responses to emergencies for posterity.

Chiefly to replay at lab parties, conventions, and research symposia.

What better way is there to show you care than by replaying your friends', coworkers', and competitors' reactions to the unexpected, over and over?[11]

Notes to self (and others):

1. *This is no joke.*[2]
2. *Although it may still be funny.*[3]
3. *Especially if it's happening to someone other than you.*[4]
4. *Most especially if they deserved it.*
5. *And a fire extinguisher.*
6. *As a Paratechnologist, you should have the pockets, or pocket dimensions, for them.*[7]
7. *Assuming they weren't volatilized as well.*
8. *In addition to a new assistant.*
9. *And possibly new glasses.*
10. *Particularly if there is room for them all.*
11. *And over.*

EXPLOSIONS HAPPEN

No matter how vast your intellect, no matter how complete or proven your theories, no matter how advanced your simulations, no matter how total your comprehension, no matter what computational resources you have access to or create, no one limited mind or intelligence contains the totality of actuality.

Despite your best efforts, predictions, and preparations, things will blow up.

Often in your face.

Your eyes will be clouded by soot.
    Your ears will ring.
    Lights will flash before your eyes.
    You will lose track of your surroundings.
    You may crash into nearby objects.
    You will get hurt.
    Your dreams will crumble around you.

You may even burn your mustache.

Dust yourself off.
   Put out any fires.[1]
   Clean up the mess.
   Make certain everyone is okay.[2]
   Try again.

That's all you can do.

Do everything within your power to meet with success because, inevitably, you will fail. Failure, however, can become your greatest motivation, your greatest opportunity, and your greatest incentive to grow and progress.[3]

Notes to self (and others):

1. *On yourself first.*
2. *Not necessarily in this order.*
3. *I hope you are fortunate enough to experience explosions of insight only. Most other explosions are not quite as enjoyable.[4]*
4. *Or productive.*

ON SELECTING A RESEARCH TOPIC

There are more questions waiting to be answered in the macroverse than there are grains of sand distributed through all the heavens.[1]

Why is it then that so many young Gnomes have difficulty deciding on an intellectual pursuit to dedicate themselves to addressing?

Lack of imagination?
Lack of insight?
Lack of understanding?
Lack of opportunity?

No.

The root of their initial problems is most often a lack of passion!

This is not to say that young, aspiring Paratechnologists do not have passion. Rather, young, aspiring Paratechnologists have yet to find the question they are passionate about.[2]

• • •

This, unfortunately, is not a question I can find or answer for you.

I can, however, tell you that once you have found the question you most want answered, many more will follow and you will embark upon the most joyous quest of your life… that of discovery.

Notes to self (and others):

1. *Or my sheets after a visit to the beach.*
2. *And this question is not "how not to answer any more questions," for that is the path to ultimate endings.[3]*
3. *Or boredom.[4]*
4. *Unless you are seeking to cultivate a sense of alert attention which disallows boredom and leaves open the door for unending curiosity and exploration, albeit via a different path.[5]*
5. *But I digress.*

MAKING YOUR RESEARCH YOUR OWN (AND WHETHER YOU LET IT FALL INTO THE HANDS OF OTHERS)

This is really simple.

There are essentially two types of Paratechnologists:

Those who share and those who do not.

Will you selflessly work for the betterment of Gnomekind, for the furtherance of knowledge without regard to reward, and for your ideals?[1]

Or will you be a maverick, putting yourself ahead of your fellow Gnomes and striving for excellence motivated only by your own concerns, interests, and desires?[2]

To put the question another way, do you put yourself before others or others before yourself?

There is plenty of room in the greater multiverse for both types of Paratechnologists. Neither is right or wrong. But you will end up being largely one or the other.

Now is your moment of truth. If you have not done so already, now is your time to decide.

What type of Paratechnologist will you be?

There is no false dichotomy here… only your choice.[3]

Notes to self (and others):

1. *Knowing your own needs will be provided for by the larger Gnomish community and support superstructure, and you will be rewarded on the journey.*
2. *Understanding that your own contributions benefit everyone as much as yourself.*
3. *Deciding if, when, and how you share information becomes rather academic (and insignificant) after this point.*[4]
4. *Okay, maybe there is a false dichotomy but this doesn't change your decision or your need to make one.*

WHY YOU NEED A TOOL BELT

So you don't lose your tools![1]

There is always work to be done. Thus there should always be tools at hand.
    This logic is irrefutable.[2]

Say you don't fancy a tool belt.
    Then carry a toolbox.

So carrying a toolbox throws your back out of alignment, puts calluses on your palms, throws off your research strut, tweaks your shoulder, and causes your arms to ache.
    Now is your opportunity!
    Why not build a hovering toolbox that responds to voice commands? Maybe a personal pocket dimension for storing all your Paratechnological devices that anticipates your every need? What about bottomless pockets with interior searchlights and integrated fishing lines to hook, catch, and reel in desired gear? Maybe a modified fishing vest, incorporating small, hand-

sized color-coded teleportation portals to allow you to reach through and grab desired tools from specified locations in your workshop?

You are a Paratechnologist! Surely you can come up with a solution!

Also, tool belts are cool.[3]

Notes to self (and others):

1. *Isn't that obvious?*
2. *Unless you diligently try to refute it.*
3. *See* Fashion, Flash, and Flare and Why You Want Them.

SHINY IS BETTER

You are not done when you think you are done.

This is one of the principal rules of your Craft.

When you think you are done, your work has just begun.[1]

When you think you are done, the fun has just begun.[2]

After your latest creation finally achieves your desired aim(s), remember that a little decoration goes a long way, and a lot of decoration goes even further.

Add those bells and whistles! Add whistles to your bells and bells to your whistles!
   Extra cogs, widgets, doohickeys, and you-name-its are *NOT* unnecessary! They are the very soul of your art!

So, embellish, exaggerate, and explore!

Let your work shine![3]

<u>*Notes to self (and others):*</u>

1. *I recommend keeping that rhyme in your mind all the time.*
2. *This is an alternative, or much appreciated complement, to the above.*
3. *And make it shinier!*

DESIGN CONSIDERATIONS TO ADDRESS

So, your creation is shiny, but is it shiny *enough*?

Just because you have taken your idea to the limit does not mean it cannot be taken further.

After all, does the horizon not extend beyond your point of view?

Does invention end with the completion of one idea?

Is more not more and even more not even more?

Before finalizing your work, questions to resolve include:

Is your creation burnished enough?

If not, polish, chrome, and finish away!

Are multiple redundancies included?

When in doubt, add another failsafe, duplicate, or back-up!

Are these redundancies redundant?

If not, add more!

Have you completely utilized the entirety of the color palette on your invention?

Aside from bright lights, shimmering surfaces, and explosions, nothing draws attention like a lot of color!

Are there any ideas (or objects) that have yet to be added to your device that could be?

Here is your chance to find a place for an idea that has yet to find a worthy home: shoeless shoehorns, anti-strobing strobe lights, antiplaque dental forcefields, self-cleaning hats, foot deodorant, and lintless shirts rejoice!

Alternatively, this is your chance to get rid of some less than desirable objects that you might have lying around. Those handmade earlobe muffs given to you by your Great-Great-Aunt Spoolspindler might finally find a worthy re-embodiment!

Are there any discoveries that you have made or novel technical applications that you have uncovered that could conceivably be added to this device (or others)?

There is no better way to make something better than by adding something better!

Is your creation sleek and efficient?

If so, consider adding more thingamabobs, doohickeys, gizmos, and whatnots.[1]

Does your contraption push the bounds of any theories?

If not, start looking for borders to push and lines to cross![2]

· · ·

What senses is your device NOT engaging?

Perhaps it needs to belch, whistle, whirl, flash, burp, fluctuate, or flare.

Finally, does your invention include any surprises?

Who doesn't love a good surprise?[3]

Notes to self (and others):

1. *All technical terms.*
2. *Especially those of convention.*
3. *What could be more exciting or satisfying than seeing the look of shock on someone's face as something unexpected happens that you knew you had a hand in creating?*

HOW NOT TO PRODUCE (OR BE PRODUCTIVE) – A RALLYING CALL AGAINST IDLENESS

You are a Paratechnologist.

Your purpose lies in seeking and understanding the vast unknown, shaping the unknowable, molding the possible to your vision, heightening the overall level of emergent intelligence in the multiverse, and creating substance from empyrean ideals.

Do not let mere distraction break your focus!

The heights of Paratechnological fame and reward that will be yours for the taking, recognition of your untold benefits to Gnomekind, offers of feathered hats, mirrored goggles, dashing scarves, and shiny capes, free lunches and speaking engagements, all these and more will beckon as your knowledge, results, and prestige grow.

Resist the temptation to idleness!

Create a subroutine in your Abstract to fill in for you![1]

·   ·   ·

Fight the urge to pontificate![2]
    Let your work speak for itself!

Do not wallow in free gifts and tributes to the greatness of your mind and its works.[3]
    Let the well-oiled cogs and wheels of your cognition churn ever onward and forward!

Your destiny lies elsewhere.

Go to your lab.
    The next great idea awaits!

<u>*Notes to self (and others):*</u>

1. *It can even bring back the leftovers.*
2. *Granted, this can be a bit difficult for Gnomes.*
3. *Odds are, you'll be able to create more interesting gizmos than those you're given.*

FASHION, FLASH, AND FLARE – AND WHY YOU WANT THEM

Many Paratechnologists are extravagant. Others are dashing. Still others are dazzling. A few are even ostentatious.[1,3]

I say they are not showy enough.

A Paratechnologist who does not stand out in a crowd is a Paratechnologist who has no sense of proportion, no sense of style.
    They might as well be invisible.

Paratechnologists need verve.
    Paratechnologists brim with zest.
    Paratechnologists radiate pizzazz.
    Paratechnologists epitomize élan.

As a Paratechnologist, your very presence is an expression of how you feel, how you think, and how you act.

. . .

Paratechnologists *are* flash.
    Paratechnologists *embody* flare.

As a Paratechnologist, if you are not eye-catching enough to draw the attention of your enemies away from your clockwork devices, allies, various minions, and attendant automatons, how can you expect for your devices and friends to have the freedom to operate most effectively?

As a Paratechnologist, if onlookers do not have to shield their eyes[4] when their gaze falls upon you, how else will you dazzle them with your wit?

As a Paratechnologist, if your very presence does not garner a sense of awe and wonder, who else will inspire your fellows to the heights of intellection and amazement?

As a Paratechnologist, if you don't dazzle, what will?

Paratechnologists wear how they feel.
    Paratechnologists express the heights of their ideas, the depths of their imagination, the completeness of their technical and theoretical understanding, through their garments, accouterments, decorations, appurtenances, embellishments, and adornments.[5]

You are your kit.

Get accessorizing!

. . .

Notes to self (and others):

1. *To be considered ostentatious by other Paratechnologists is saying something.*[2]
2. *Not necessarily good.*
3. *To be considered ostentatious by non-Paratechnologists is expected.*
4. *Or scratch their heads.*
5. *For inspiration, I suggest either Bundera Granquaria's comprehensive* Elements of Style – The Gnomish Perspective on Cultural, Ideological, and Personal Expression *or Muerdiune's insightful* Garment Augmentation and Accessorization.

GREAT THINGS GO GREAT TOGETHER

Unless they do not.[1]

This is a fundamental guiding principle of Paratechnology.[2]

There are few exceptions to this rule.[4]

In fact, the more great things you employ or incorporate, the greater potential for your invention.

For example, you have designed a self-organized, self-integrating, self-assembling biocompatible nano-composite neural network that merges with the wearer's nervous system to allow direct interface with the Gnomosphere while simultaneously providing seamless mental control of Paratechnological devices. You have also created a mutable polymorphic polychromatic self-applicable tattoo that can be redesigned by the bearer at their whim, its expression only limited by their imagination.

Why not combine the two devices into one?

Why not use your greatest inventions and ideas to mutually reinforce, augment, and supplement one another?

Your fellow Paratechnologists (and innocent bystanders, witnesses, and members of the local media) will thank you for it.

Notes to self (and others):

1. *An exciting potential avenue of research unto itself.*
2. *Insofar as Paratechnology has any guiding principles that are not entirely fabricated or made up on the fly to suit the author's whim or the changing dictates of a given situation.[3]*
3. *For more detail and further stimulation, I suggest Heartwhistle Handcrank's* Making Stuff Up: The Art and Science.
4. *Treat each exception as the wondrous discovery that it is! Examples that I have discovered include but are not limited to: porridge, milk and orange juice, instructions and toys (almost any set of instructions with almost any toy),vanilla ice cream and mustard, torches and bunnies (especially arming said bunnies with torches), hot tea and mayonnaise, rain jackets composed of absorbent materials, and others.[5]*
5. *Other nonlimiting examples include listening and arguments, socks and soup, katanas and Gnomes, antigravity devices and paperweights, fire and research notes, Dwarven guests and leftovers (at least if you hope to have any), dragons and generosity, squirrels and straight lines, and crackers and whistling, to name but a few.[6]*
6. *In truth, the list of great things that don't go great together could be the subject of several other entire volumes.[7]*
7. *I'm working on a complete set.[8]*
8. *A new avenue of Paratechnological research!*

ON AUGMENTATION, SELF-BETTERMENT, AND PERSONAL TRANSFORMATION

Expect the best.[1]

That way you can make it happen.

As a Paratechnologist, you are uniquely suited to actualizing your vision.[2]

Choose a good one, one worth pursuing and bringing to fruition, one that provides a challenge for yourself, and furthers the development and depth of your Art.

In my day, I have seen innumerable expressions of Gnomish ingenuity and imagination. Examples include Gnomes taking forms ranging between rainbow-hued dragons, intelligent energy clouds, distributed intelligence matrices, living, lightning-emblazoned clouds, self-sustaining stars, independent pocket dimensions, cohesive nanoswarms, sessile, coralesque extrusions, models of the multiverse, planetary systems, and favorite galaxies, floating thought crystals, fey creatures from faeries to Elven kings, spaceships and other vessels, angelic and daemonic figures and beasts, and myriad plants and animals—to name but a few.

Though wondrous, these are but outward physical manifestations. With personal transformations so vast, imagine what is possible with your mind, your awareness, your perception, your intelligence, and your understanding!

Then consider what other marvels you will be able to create through the joining of the two!

As a Paratechnologist, you will define your own limits.

Any expressions of your Paratechnological aspirations can be yours.

Make your dreams a reality! This is, after all, the primary vocation of the Paratechnologist.

With the appropriate groundwork laid, reach for the heavens! Your mind and body will be the bridge.

Notes to self (and others):

1. _If you cannot, then you might consider changing professions. Otherwise, with all the difficulties you will face throughout your career as a Paratechnologist, why bother?_
2. _Which is why it is exceedingly important that you have one (or, even better, many)._

ON THE PROPER DISPOSITION OF YOUR MINIONS

What are your aims as a Paratechnologist?

How can you most effectively and efficiently achieve your desired ends?

What projects are you currently managing or hoping to start?

What resources do you need to accomplish your goals?

Are you faced with any resource allocation limitations?

Do you have any free time?

Would you like some?

All of these questions and more can be addressed with the proper disposition of minions.[1]

I follow a very simple strategy when it comes to organizing, creating, and recruiting my miniature (and not so miniature) assistants and aids:

Get the most for the least.[5]

That way, everyone is most likely to be happy, most especially yourself.

Notes to self (and others):

1. *Curiously, having minions also results in a steady propagation of other questions such as:*
2. *Where did all these things come from?*
3. *Do my minions actually listen to me—or anyone else for that matter?*
4. *Is all this trouble worth it?*
5. *Who is going to clean all this up?*
6. *Why do I even try?*[2]
7. *If you are looking for a life without challenge (or excitement),one filled with quietude and seclusion, then utilizing minions in whatever form is not recommended (nor for that matter is Paratechnology). If, however, you are seeking unending opportunity to work creatively in a dynamic setting filled with daily challenges, then you have found a wonderful outlet through your utilization of minions, automatons, clockwork devices, and other hired and unhired help.*[3]
8. *Especially when one considers how much you work for their benefit.*[4]
9. *Remember, there is a fine line to be walked between satisfying your minions and satisfying yourself.*
10. *And no, I am not being parsimonious.*[6]
11. *This principle is also known as Occlusion's Razor.*[7]
12. *Occlusion was a Gnome well known for cutting himself with razors that were a bit too keen.*

MAKING THE MOST OF A BAD—OR, MORE LIKELY, DESPERATE—SITUATION

Events do not always go your way. Nor does circumstance always unfold as expected.

You have just completed your magnum opus on the transubstantiation of goat yogurt when your Abstract is thrust through a dimensional tear of your own (perhaps accidental) making.

What do you do?

Hopefully, you've backed up your body-mind state data and your Abstract within the Construct or an ancillary Abstract. If not, you brave the unknown realms of the dimensional tear and recover it.

Who knows, you might discover your next research topic.

There is a firm knock at your door. You look around in confusion because you don't have a door. You have a multidimensional access port that changes position depending on your whim.

Who could be knocking at your door?

Investigating the situation, you discover that an elder daemon has come looking for the part of its wing that you collected to be sublimated as a reaction component in an alchemical transformation to create an ointment for use when you need pigs to fly.

You invite the daemon in for tea and offer it a pair of magically augmented hyperglider wing extensions with flaming tips and speakers to play menacing theme music upon command.

The daemon leaves happy.

You have made a new friend.

You get a missive marked "Urgent." Opening the letter reveals a holographic representation from the family of your former research partner asking you to rescue him from the clutches of a mysterious cabal intent on extracting the secrets of his mother's mushroom stew.

You agree to help.

You bring a bowl of his mother's mushroom stew to the cabal. They innocently take the stew and partake of it heartily. After sampling, those still conscious willingly return your friend and no longer request the recipe.

In gratitude for your efforts, your friend shares the recipe with you. After a bit of analysis, you use the stew as highly efficient rocket fuel.

After exhaustive research, extensive effort, and vigorous simulation, you are achingly close to reconstructing a working scale model of a long-lost Gnomish floating sky warren from meticulously gathered lint, dust, debris, and wood fragments, as part of your final project in Clockworks 101, when your roommate comes in and turns on the overhead fan, scattering your carefully assembled stacks of detritus to the far reaches of your dorm room.

How do you react?

With a flick of your wrist, you put your roommate into a stasis field while your Abstract quickly disengages the fan's systems.

The air calm, the room quiet, you now have time to finish your work undisturbed.

Life is full of surprises.

. . .

Welcome them.[1,3]

Notes to self (and others):

1. *Unless, of course, the surprise happens to be defective. Then consider sending it back. A defective surprise can ruin an event or surprise party.*[2]
2. *If you are devious, however, I would suggest keeping even defective surprises. A faulty surprise can be even more exciting than a working one.*
3. *For a comprehensive overview of how to make it through more sticky situations than can be found in an army of confectioner's nightmares, I cannot recommend* Gnomercy - The Uniquely Gnomish Art of Doing Whatever It Takes to Survive *highly enough. In this exhaustive, interactive tome, not only will you find an unrivaled host of calamitous situations that you should hope to never have to endure, you will also be able to download the necessary skills, techniques, and knowledge required to survive them.*[4]
4. *Also, you will find quite a bit of useful cooking advice.*

WHEN NOT TO JUMP TO CONCLUSIONS

Generally when located near a precipice, without access to magic or appropriate device, jumping to conclusions is a bad idea.[1]

Being prepared, understanding a situation and its attendant problems, modes of operation, and governing laws, attending to the niceties of a given condition, following routes of possibility and their potential expression, anticipating errors and their resolution, modeling uncertainties and solutions... these are the requisite steps for the leaps in understanding that allow one to jump to conclusions.

Safely.

This foresight prepares the ground of intellection, sowing the seeds of ideation, allowing the mind and its associated thoughts and creations to flourish.

Then, leaps in understanding happen of their own accord, guided toward desired ends, often bringing forth rewards far greater than ever anticipated.

Notes to self (and others):

1. *Unless of course one is testing a theory or proving a point.[2]*
2. *Or if all your friends are doing it.[3]*
3. *In this case, however, adequately modeling the situation or sharing a suitable simulation is preferred to actual jumping.[4]*
4. *Unless you're doing it just for the fun of it.*

PLANNING FOR SUCCESS (WHILE ACCEPTING FAILURE)

Paratechnology is chock full of idealism, theory, esoterica, anti-obfuscation, wondrous absurdities, realization, insight, revelation, the highest strivings imaginable by sentient beings[1], continual refinement, discovery, and mostly honest assessments of reality, our work, our selves, and our likelihood of success.[2]

Unfortunately, Paratechnology is just as full of failure (if not more so).

Failure, and the mistakes made from it, are the very raging fiery catapult of furious innovation propelling our luminous collective understanding forward in erratic fits and starts through ever-continual improvements in knowledge and experience.

The future is built on failure.

Do not reject it, run away from it, or deny its utility and power.

. . .

Failure, then, is merely a matter of perspective... a view to be used and appreciated, but not one that should limit or otherwise constrain your work or endeavors.

Even in failure, there is a kernel of success.

This brings us to one of the most fundamental equations in all of Paratechnology:

$$F = ma$$

Where F is the future, m is the mind, and a is aspiration.

Put your mind to work and the future will follow!

Notes to self (and others):

1. *At least that we've come up with or happened upon so far.*
2. *Not to mention self-deprecating humor.*

IN THE COMPANY OF PARATECHNOLOGISTS

Be yourself.[1]

Although given to excess, abstraction, eccentricity, absent-mindedness, care-lessness, forgetfulness, esoterica, neglect, ridiculousness, and delusion, Parat-echnologists are a fairly perceptive lot.

We are generally wise and observant enough to see through pretension, connivance, and obfuscation.

Do yourself a favor and save us the extra work of sorting through any nonsense (real or feigned).[3] We'll all work better together that way.

As a Paratechnologist, you will get quite a bit more accomplished working in the company of honest friends and respectful colleagues than among rivals and enemies.

Plus, friends are fun.[4]

Notes to self (and others):

1. *Unless you're working hard to not be yourself.*[2]
2. *Then don't be yourself. Choose what you want to be.*
3. *Don't try to be odder than you are. Oddity will come in time. Let it.*
4. *Who better to appreciate your pranks and jibes?*

CHOOSING APPROPRIATE FACIAL HAIR

Despite what any non-Gnome may tell you, choosing appropriate facial coiffure is one of the single most momentous decisions of your career... each day.[1]

Thankfully, there are more types of facial hair styles than there are days of the year. Whether sculpted by hand or imbued by magic, this variety gives even the most finicky and mercurial of Paratechnologists every opportunity to select a style amenable to their taste, predilections, and propensity to catch on fire.[2]

I suggest a practical approach to facial styling. That is to say, select a style appropriate to your needs. Although far from complete in scope, the following concise list includes a smattering of the myriad options awaiting your discerning eye and keenest perspective:

The Beard Nest or Treasure Trove is ideally suited to capturing and storing food and other items. This style is especially appropriate for those wanting extra storage or portability.

For the gastroGnome, the Shovel assists in guiding food to mouth and catching what might have been missed but otherwise desired.

For the Paratechnologist always wanting a spare hand or an extra set of digits, the Hydra will facilitate manipulating objects with its branching network of moving appendages. The Hydra is also particularly suited to dangerous tasks—for when it is damaged, more than one tendril returns to take the damaged hairs' place![4]

The Conqueror—with its vicious blade-like mien to intimidate foes, shake rivals, and inspire loyalty in allies—is well suited to the Paratechnologist keen on moving up in the world.[5]

Often chosen by those with a cosmological bent, the Nebulae is much admired for its beatific shifting forms reminiscent of stellar bodies and inter-stellar clouds.[7]

Held in high esteem by idealized engineers, the Spark exhibits flashes of randomized electrical patterning inspired by arcs of lightning and other ener-getic manifestations. This 'stache shows you mean business, that you have a certain verve and zest, and that you pack quite a punch.[8]

For the abstruse or intentionally arcane, the Eccentric—with its inherent obscurity, studied disregard, and occasional self-importance—will cloud you in a fog of oddity that only the brightest and most persistent will be able to penetrate.

As a very playful style, the Smoke Plume, with its irregular vertical columns and cumulohairus puffs, will inspire many an open-ended conver-sation.[9]

For the mercurial, the Reaction—with its subtle transitions shifting back and forth from one form to another depending on surrounding conditions, variables, and raw materials—can be the perfect choice.[10]

A beard without end, the Multiverse, with its riotously incomprehensible multidimensional forms, will inspire more pondering than your cherished mother-in-law's cooking.[11]

Particularly prized by notional physicists and archmathematicians, the Theoretician shifts between your favorite equations per your whims and subconscious desires.[12]

Recondite and indecipherable, the Thinker will give even a noeticist pause.

For those Gnomes who take their detective work seriously, the PI gets the job done, no questions asked. Thick and rugged, often accompanied by a roguish hat or rakishly buttoned shirt, the PI means action.

In contrast to the PI, the Mullet is for Gnomes who are *not* all business. In point of fact, the Mullet is all business in the front and a party in the back.

For the Gnome who disdains social convention, the Mountain Gnome or

Mad Gnome are the neck fros for you. Prized for their wanton freedom and inherent wildness, either the Mountain Gnome or the Mad Gnome is the ideal option for Gnomes who will not be contained!

You have many great choices to make in your most eminent career-to-be. Don't let choosing the wrong beard or mustache hold you back.

Notes to self (and others):

1. *Thankfully it is one choice that can also be rectified quite easily if chosen in a moment of weakness or poor judgment.*
2. *See for instance Gregario the Luxuriant's illuminating* Mustache Compendium and Facial Opus *for more details on facial styles, grooming, and maintenance.*[3]
3. *Also, peruse the illustrations for quite a few laughs.*
4. *Be forewarned, however, this mustache and/or beard can rapidly get out of control if allowed to respawn too frequently.*
5. *Especially in bureaucratic circles which, by many a sage's estimation, may be far removed from actually moving anywhere.*[6]
6. *At least worthwhile.*
7. *Avoid those featuring singularities, quasars, supernovas, and the like. They are more trouble than they are worth and will seriously dampen your social style.*
8. *The Spark can also be used to restart many common objects, which comes in quite handy in more situations than you may care to know.*
9. *Be careful not to employ a rendition that is too realistic, as you are likely to get doused—repeatedly—especially at parties. In fact, this has been known to become quite the rage at large events.*
10. *Just don't let it get too close to any important experiments.*
11. *It can also be more ponderous than her leftovers.*
12. *The Theoretician can also be quite helpful in calling forth figures you may have forgotten, or in capturing particularly clever ideas for posterity.*

KEEPING YOUR INSIGHTS, DISCOVERIES, AND ATTAINMENTS IN CONTEXT

You should always endeavor to be superior, to improve, and to achieve beyond even your expectations. This is the path of development as a Paratechnologist.

Though the path of the Paratechnologist is fraught with challenge, often treacherous, filled with many nonlinear convolutions, multidimensional twists, formidable abstractions, and enchanting baubles, you must always push forward, lest your knowledge and abilities stultify, languish, or degenerate.

To do otherwise invites your limitations.

To accept opens the possibility of discovery.

And this, then, is your resolution and opportunity.

Ever look forward. Ever seek for what must be done this instant that you may prosper and flourish in the next.

Do not compare the self of this instant or its accomplishments against ones from the past, for the you of yore is irrevocably gone, a universe extinguished, never to be revived in its myriad imperfections, foibles, grand visions, and triumphs. There is only the you of the moment, making the most of the present, fostering and uplifting your future incarnation.

Your future is realized by your choices and mindset at each twinkling and every juncture.

Although the temptation may be strong, neither should you compare your evolution and achievements against those of others.[1] Every being is participating in his, her, or its own journey. Where other lives lead, what their quests uncover, will be left to their actions, decisions, and desires.

Never let others' deficiencies and imperfections become your own.[2]

With a bit of humility, an open, inquisitive mind, a desire to persevere and grow, a healthy respect for your limitations and failings, an honest awareness of self and others, and an abiding appreciation for the wonders of the macroverse's unfolding, all is feasible, the least of which is your improvement and continued development.

When in doubt, keep your mind open and your mouth closed.[4]

Notes to self (and others):

1. *Especially if you meet with particular success or someone you meet is especially dashing.*
2. *Just as your own mistakes provide chances to learn, so, too, can those of others.[3]*
3. *Unless of course you're laughing at those shortcomings. Then you might as well enjoy yourself and worry about learning later.*
4. *An especially difficult proposition for a Paratechnologist. The mouth-closing, that is.*

WHEN YOUR PEER REVIEW NEEDS TO BE RE-REVIEWED

Great minds do not think alike.[1]

Your ideas are yours and yours alone. Sharing your ideas, your findings, your discoveries, and your insights, can be painful.

Expect criticism. Expect disagreement from your peers. Anticipate failure. All these will follow, precede, and foreshadow your research career.

No matter how tempting, never give in to bad advice or unwarranted criticism.[4] Have the strength and resolution to persevere through adversity, that your triumphant idea may see the light of day.

Who knows?
   With a bit of luck, your great idea may be the next frictionless toothpick, toiletless toilet paper, touchless nose hair trimmer, Dwarf-proof beard mower, snore muter, or anti-antibacterial soap.

. . .

Notes to self (and others):

1. *Some great minds don't think at all!*[2]
2. *Although those types of minds would not consider themselves great.*[3]
3. *Or consider much at all for that matter.*
4. *If criticism is warranted, then seize upon the welcome opportunity to improve your work.*

AVOIDING DELUSION (ESPECIALLY YOUR OWN!)

Truth[1] must be held in perspective, examined from every angle, surveyed for imperfections, gaps, and opportunities.

Perspectives change, as does understanding.

There is no final point from which to judge truth.

There is no absolute perspective from which to judge knowledge.

As a Paratechnologist, your job, your purpose, is to take truth[2,] and its myriad expressions in reality, and examine them from as many angles as possible; to think of new perspectives from which to examine and understand truth; and then implement and further that understanding.

Once you have a grasp of truth, in whatever form, you must seize hold of it with all your might, clasp it within your grasp, squeezing it, compressing it further and further until it densifies infinitely creating an inescapable gravity-well in space-time drawing yet more knowledge and understanding within its inexorable clutches... finally collapsing inward, awaiting ultimate rebirth as a new universe of knowledge.[3]

Once you have taken hold of truth, in any form worthy of pursuit, you must shatter its confines to the farthest heavens, releasing its echoes to the very limits of the macroverse, its chorus radiating through and encompassing other ideas within its totality, extending the limits of the known, enfolding the unknown within its vibrant embrace.[5,6]

From a personal standpoint, your task is *not* to impose your own sense of importance, self-aggrandizement, pride (whether deserved or undeserved), or sense of self-worth on the topic or result of your analysis.[7]

This very act will cloud your perspective and resulting understanding.[9]

Which will further divorce you from truth[11] and its understanding.

And nobody wants a divorce.[12]

Notes to self (and others):

1. *Including accepted, understood, and relative truths.*
2. *Both relative and absolute truth.*
3. *Or some permutation thereof.[4]*
4. *See, for example, Hossenfelder and Smolin's* Conservative solutions to the black hole information problem *for a brief, elementary discussion of the fate of black holes, the birth of baby universes from singularities, along with implications for space-time.*
5. *And there you have two of life's greatest joys in a simple nutshell. As a Paratechnologist you should always strive to do one of two things:*
6. *smash things, or*
7. *blow them up.*
8. *And what could be more exciting than an explosion that resonates throughout the megacosm (or, at minimum, one that reverberates through your entire mind-state)?*
9. *The macroverse does not care whether you discovered the latest waxless mustache polisher... no matter how shiny it makes your 'stache![8]*

10. *That's what your family and friends are for! They will sing your praises for you and the macroverse through them.*
11. *And, after all this, I really hope you understand.*[10]
12. *If not, you can always re-read, transfer an updated mind-state, ask for help, or improve your cognitive faculties.*
13. *Including but not limited to accepted, understood, relative, and absolute truths.*
14. *Granted, some people, beings, entities, substrates, modalities, states, and intelligences do in fact want divorces but that wouldn't help my point now would it?*

STICKS AND STONES MAY BREAK MY BONES
BUT RANTS WILL NEVER BOTHER ME

As a Paratechnologist, you are (or will be) something of an academic.

Certainly you will have adventures.

Most assuredly your projects and experiments will have a heady mix of excitement and danger.

Without a doubt your very presence will rock the heavens![1]

But, when the day is done, you will blend your adventuring, exploratory, and innovative ways with those of the academic and scholar.

This does not mean you will be bland!
    The Omnispark forbid!
    But you may have to deal with those who are.

As a theoretician-cum-scientist-cum-magician-cum-scholar-cum-technol-ogist-cum-researcher-cum-resident-eccentric you will also have to deal with more than your fair share of questions and criticisms.[2]

Often these comments will be of a personal nature.

Don't take said criticisms personally or make them personal.

Take the questions of your peers, the vehemence of would-be foes, and the barbs of detractors for what they are: your good fortune!

Heated questions, volatile comments, rude remarks, and snide disparage-ments are all to your good fortune!

Your good fortune to explain something that is little understood.

Your good fortune to elucidate a matter that has been unresolved.

Your good fortune to enlighten and inspire.

Your good fortune to fill a need.

Your good fortune to better and improve.

Your good fortune to be in a position to answer the call and wage war against ignorance and imperfect understanding.

· · ·

Your good fortune to move forward.

Know your detractors, your naysayers, your opponents, your areas of study, your work, and yourself.[3]

Know how to make your critics understand, and you will make yourself better and your work more likely to meet with success.[6]

Notes to self (and others):

1. *Often explosively.*
2. *As a Paratechnologist, you will meet with quite a bit of both. Best be prepared.*
3. *Tack this on to what you need to know for Paratechnological work and this is quite a bit to know.[4]*
4. *But I know you can do it—after all, you're a Paratechnologist![5]*
5. *Just don't be a know-it-all. We have enough of those.*
6. *Also, you will probably meet with quite a lot of bad food at the meetings with the aforementioned critics, commentators, experts, expositors, and pundits. Best keep a discerning eye lest your stomach regret it.*

WHY YOU NEED A SIDEKICK

One of the many beauties of being a Paratechnologist is that dearest allies, closest assistants, and valued companions don't have to be earned.

They can be created.

Not only can your companions be created, they can be formed to meet your every need, vicissitude, and whim.

They can be fashioned to perform tasks that you are unable or incapable of performing yourself.

They can be generated to excel at endeavors you do not wish to perform or that you have not yet augmented yourself to complete.

They can be produced to help you grow and become better.

They can be made to fit your sense of style and augment your very presence.

They can even be fashioned to enjoy your company.[1,2]

Practically, given the exigencies of research in action—often hazardous field-work, resource capture, recovery, recruitment expeditions, and day-to-day adventures—sidekicks can prove invaluable.

They can provide cover, suppressive fire, or shielding to you and your companions.

They can invoke magic and incantations you are otherwise too occupied to cast yourself.

They can activate devices, mechanisms, and equipment at mission-critical times.

They can go where you cannot, do not wish to go, or are otherwise unable to go.

They can provide surveillance, intelligence, and information vital to the success of your research and associated operations.

They can offer valuable advice and alternative perspectives on finding solutions to difficult problems and intractable issues.

They can selflessly put the interests of others before their own without fear of repercussion.[4]

They can help you carry an even wider assortment of tools, mechanisms, gadgets, gear, and instrumentation.

They can set up camp and prepare meals while you regale your comrades with tales of bravery and feats of strength.[5]

They can rub your feet and massage your back after a long day on the march, in the saddle, or hunched over an ancient dusty tome.

They can help add to, clean, polish, and organize your collection of gears, ball bearings, parts, springs, pulleys, and machines.

They can even offer grooming and styling advice.[6]

The real question becomes, why would you want only one?

Also, who else is going to play your theme music?

Notes to self (and others):

1. *As hard as this may be to believe.*
2. *This may put them ahead of most of your family members by default.[3]*
3. *I'm just throwing that out as a possibility... albeit an unlikely one.*

4. *Especially if they have been recently backed up, have a duplicate mind-state stored, or have an alternative replacement ready for deployment.*
5. *Or while you do your meager best to come up with interesting anecdotes to maintain the attention of more worldly adventurers.*
6. *Popular perceptions to the contrary, as a Paratechnologist, you will need* plenty *of styling advice.*

HOW TO AVOID MUSTACHE ENTANGLEMENT

Your research and various and sundry efforts in the lab, along with endeavors in realms theoretical, practical, and actual, are of paramount importance. Often, you cannot afford interruptions, disruptions, delays, or error. In a word (or two), you cannot afford mustache entanglement.

Insofar as I am aware, there is no greater single threat to Paratechnological advancement than this dire prospect.

Many Gnomes quaver in fear at the mere thought.

Others are wracked by paralysis at the simple consideration.

A few of my dearest colleagues have been knocked into raging stupors when faced with this dire calamity.

I will ask you this, *is jeopardizing your future work worth the risk?*[1]

Only you can perform the multivariate analyses, modeling, and simulations necessary to determine the answer to your satisfaction.[2]

I will, however, offer this: there is a reason most Paratechnologists carry a razor (or its equivalent) at all times.[4]

Notes to self (and others):

1. *Consider wisely… the fate of the multiverse may depend upon your answer.*
2. *I suggest that you do the math* **before** *any emergency. During the crisis it will be far too late.[3]*
3. *Also, be sure to double-check your calculations.*
4. *And we know how to wield it![5]*
5. *The Omnispark forbid any stray hairs get in our way! Of course, I am hardly one to talk.[6]*
6. *I myself carry a holographic antiextruder (professional model, platinum series), a mustache evaporator (Alchemists' preferred edition), an automated beard mower Mark X with dual backup engines and self-guidance heuristics, a multispectrum laser trimmer with hands-free targeting system, an autonomous, self-actuated beard bot, a 'stache dissoluter, a field enclosed hand-held plasma torch, and, when all else fails, a straight razor.*

ON CLEANING UP (AND KEEPING CLEAN)

A few words on hygiene[1] and upkeep.

You want to be *shiny*.
>You want to have a certain je ne sais quoi.[2]
>You want to ooze technomagical chic.
>You want to be the envy of the adventure set.

Then for Light's sake, clean up!

Use your beard mower and whisker glosser!
>Dust off your eyebrow trimmer and ear hair comber!
>Engage your snout polisher and nose hair detangler!
>Don your sports goggles and ear-restraining helmet!
>Scrape, burnish, pneumatic drill, and scrub your teeth!
>Clean out the wax repositories impairing your hearing!
>Shower, sonicate, volatilize, employ nanofields, or otherwise clean last year's experimental residue off yourself!

Shine your belt buckles and furbish your nanocomposite clothing!
Sandblast your toenails and prune your fingernails!
Put on some boots—without holes!
Take care of yourself! [3]

Just because you're a mad scientist—ahem, Paratechnologist—doesn't mean you have to look like it!

Notes to self (and others):

1. *And I am not talking about chemical or industrial hygiene, although those apply here as well.*
2. *Actually I do know. It's why I wrote this tome.*
3. *The same general principles apply to your lab. Follow them.*

YOUR LEGACY

Will pale in comparison to the wondrous totality that is the greater macro-verse.[1]

And, in truth, that is something to be proud of in and of itself.

This leads us to a simple truth: no matter how great your creations[5], there will always be something greater to strive for, some new idea to test, some new theory to posit, some new realm to explore[6], some new material to uncover or generate, and some new dessert to enjoy.[7]

If you do somehow become disillusioned with the marvels and possibilities presented by the limitless bounds of an ever-expanding multiverse waiting to be explored and understood, then I suggest one of the following:

1. Watch a child at play;

2. Choose a single point, object, or idea, and focus your attention on it completely until your concerns dissolve in clear, pure awareness;
3. Watch the leaves of a fern unfurl, dewdrops gather on spring leaves in the morn, or sunlight diffuse through the boughs of an untrammeled forest;
4. Slap your face solidly, hard enough to make your ears ring;
5. Transfer your consciousness to an alternate substrate capable of greater feats of cogitation and imagination;
6. Watch magical energies arise from the primordial potential;
7. Ascend to a higher realm or form of existence;[8]
8. Ask a friend what keeps them going;[9]
9. Try something completely different;
10. Take a good, long nap in the middle of a sunny day, preferably beneath the cool shade of a mature tree swaying gently in the breeze;
11. Drink a warm, palliating tea, ideally infused from hand selected freshly brewed leaves; or
12. Be brave enough to allow yourself to expire and embark on the greatest mystery of all.

With your equilibrium restored, set about creating something that will inspire others to carry on, to seek more, to be greater, and to strive for and expand upon their highest and as yet unimagined ideals.

Then you may indeed have something worthy of your pride.[10]

Notes to self (and others):

1. *And that is nothing for which to be ashamed.*[2]
2. *Unless, like the megacosm, your ego is without bound.*[3]
3. *In which case I recommend comparing the majesty of your works against the simple effectiveness of a black hole. Whoever has the greater works wins.*[4]

4. *Seek me out if you get past the first challenge. I'll find something more stimulating for round two.*

5. *And let's face it, I humbly submit, the frictionless toothpick is pretty great.*

6. *In this dimension or others, real or abstract, physical, empyreal, chimeric, or ideal.*

7. *As inventive as Paratechnologists are, confectioners, bakers, cooks, chefs, and those with growling stomachs are quite ingenious as well.*

8. *In addition to Paratechnology, Ea'ae herself and the realms beyond offer many wisdom traditions capable of setting you out on a path of personal transformation.*

9. *If you are lucky enough to have some. If not, ask yourself. If the answers you find are unsatisfactory, then consult peers, Abstracts, Constructs, experts, sages, and utilize any resources within your grasp. Then ask yourself again… until you find an answer.*

10. *And, from the great sage Mulogo's perspective, you may have inspired one less person who wants to kill you and take your stuff.*[11]

11. *In truth, from Mulogo's perspective, said person will probably still want to kill you and take your stuff, but I am a bit more optimistic than Mulogo.*[12]

12. *And, unlike Mulogo, I am a Gnome and not a wizard.*[13]

13. *But I digress.*

SEIZING OPPORTUNITY (AND WHY YOU SHOULD DIE TRYING)

I now have the privilege of trying to sum up everything I have attempted to impart in the last forty or so chapters in a succinct form that will encourage you, my dearest Paratechnological protégé, to be more than you possibly can be.[1,2]

I would be remiss to do so.

The truth of the matter is that truth cannot be summarized quickly.

Neither can Paratechnology, whose ultimate aim is to realize, understand, manipulate, alter, change, expand, tear down, transmit, express, warp, toy with, and otherwise build upon truth.[4]

Granted, the aims of Paratechnological endeavor are far-reaching, lofty, and generally accompanied by clouds of smoke, hiccups, and ducking heads, but they are indeed for you to live and discover.

In fact, I humbly submit, your time might have been better spent in your lab diagramming your next theorem, taking apart an artifact, simulating a novel material, building a prototype for your latest innovation, or desheening your forehead.[5]

In this case, having made it so far, I would ask that you put this book down and live your life unlimited—without constraint, fear, or worry, striving forward, making the most of each instance—that the fullness of the macroverse may find its expression through you and that you may expand upon the multiverse's unfolding through your discoveries, successes, and efforts.

This, then, is your chance to realize and uncover the highest of universal truths and the most practical of elemental laws, to unearth the entire range between, and to be the vehicle for all.

You have been fortunate enough to be embodied as a Paratechnologist.

Make the most of this instantiation.

May your mustache grow long and full and your Spark ever fire!

And try not to blow yourself up.[7]

Notes to self (and others):

1. *Within, outside, and beyond reason.*
2. *Being more than you can be is the way of Paratechnology... and also a clever jingle![3]*
3. *All royalties from the usage of said jingle should be directed to the Chuan Beneficence Fund, Tellanon, Ea'ae.*
4. *Perhaps Paratechnology can be summarized quickly... but then you'd miss all the fun.*
5. *Despite the perceived value in the words I impart, I would be glad if they did not fall upon your ears if this is indeed the case.[6]*
6. *My guess, however, is that were you not somehow forced to read this tome, you would be testing out the newest simulation, altered reality, synthesized experience, or other reality-expanding game.*
7. *Then you'll go far and accomplish much.[8]*
8. *If you do blow yourself up, you'll probably go far and not accomplish as much as you would have liked.*

THE GOOD STUFF: SELECT MIND-STATE ENHANCEMENTS, HEURISTICS, EMPOWERMENTS, WORLDVIEWS, SKILL SETS, TRADITIONS, & KNOWLEDGE BASES

The following rather eclectic uploads are available to improve and expand upon your assuredly already broad talents and cognoscence.[1]

I have personally gathered this information from noted sages, various respected wisdom traditions, recognized experts, noted authorities, and individuals of unsurpassed genius and ability. I can personally attest to the breadth, effectiveness, and worth of this information.

This knowledge has been entrusted to me that the macroverse will become a place ever more suitable to the highest aspirations of sentient beings.

Understand that not only will this expertise be of benefit to you but that you will be changed by its incorporation into your being.

You have been warned.[9]

The art and practice of Dwarven *Karaduen,* as taught by Kazarhan the Stout, formerly of the Home Guard.

The *Daerdaana'Duin* and associated arts of the *Doerdaana'Duin* and *Ur'Daena,* as practiced by Master Slate Flintforge, Bor'Banna.

Opening the Dragon's Gate, energy manipulation, transformation, and related arts and abilities, as discovered, expanded, and transmitted by Yip Chi Chuan, erstwhile Priest of K'un Lun.

Magic and divine energy transformation, along with the fine art of sarcasm, as practiced by Wrindanneth the Red, erstwhile Priest of Maeth Onai.

The intricacies of the *Caer'collas* and the associated arts of the Blade Singers, as disseminated by Daerdros, Master at Arms of the Home Guard.

The *Fria al'Othra*, as shared by Llyewia L'oerllana *Anuvatari Anuvaerya*.

The arts and wisdom of the *Iyela*, as preserved and maintained by Alderan, lorekeeper of the Elves of Yenaria.

The heart wisdom of the *Aeryn D'al*, as taught to the *Anuvatari* and Priests of K'un Lun.

The arts of Aeromancy, as upheld by Rowena Bowspirit, Tellanon Fleet Commander and member of the Protectorate.

The various and sundry arts of Paratechnology, as employed, discovered, understood, mocked, and utilized by Oroende, Dizzywig Paddlepulley, Whirlygig Sparksocket, Chutefunnel Knobwhistle, and Spreesprocket Goldpulley.

High magical arts, as discovered, compiled, and preserved by Éremon, Exarch of Tellanon, august Consul of the ruling Protectorate.

The wisdom and ways of the NUMEN, as developed, upheld, and practiced by Alain Ar'laen, leader of the Home Guard, Tellanon's Master-at-Arms, general, and Champion.

The tradition and lore of the *Dur'kazak*, as taught by Vaendoer Thunderhammer, member of Tellanon's ruling Protectorate and thane of the Thunderhammer clan.

The arts of theurgy and henosis, as practiced by Magdalia Miera, member of Tellanon's ruling High Council and leader of the Light's Grace congregation.

Lung-hu-i tao, inclusive of associated arts ranging from *xīnyì* to *tso-wang*, along with ancillary teachings and traditions, as transmitted by Master Wei, Yu-jen of the Priests of K'un Lun.

The ways of the *Shaur'Daus*, as employed by Raour'Saqan, Dracodaeran Lieutenant of the Home Guard.

Draconic arts and lore, as upheld and maintained by Azaelle the Golden, spawn of Auros, and Cersaegian, liege and eldest of the Fiersayne.

The way of tongues and diplomacy, as elevated by Noumel, member of the Protectorate of Tellanon.

The arts of healing and herbalism, as tendered by Salia Proventure, member of Tellanon's ruling Protectorate and Citizen advocate.

Things you just can't make up, by yours truly.

Things you wish you had made up, by Mulogo, archmage.

The subtleties of the *Wu-hsing*, as experienced by Aroganji, Fang Shih of Chang Sen.

The ways of the *Dalaren Mere*, as honored and upheld by Eidelion, *Dalaren Ka* of the Home Guard.

I'ldaerya J'al Ishentaré, as embodied by Orogast, *Jira S'al Alann*, formerly of the Home Guard.

Qìxīnquán, as practiced by Yip Chi Chuan of the K'un Lun.

The *Seura*, as danced by the *Maer'Din* of the *H'era*.

Psionic rapport, expansion, connection, and related mental arts, as discovered by EMMA the NUMEN.

The manifold ways of the *Indural*, as practiced by Goran.

The *Aurana*, as experienced by Uuraru Evensong of the *H'era Al'Marr*.

The worldsong, as experienced by the Yerens of Ea'ae.

Assorted hidden magical traditions, as cultivated by Ruena O'rein, principal magical instructor of the Home Guard and Holder of Secrets.

The arts of *Anuvatali Uraera Al'on* and other forms of augmentation, as practiced by Yrien Al'nori, member of the Home Guard

Numerous sorcerous arts along with the myriad branches of storytelling, as uncovered, transmitted, and developed by Hoyt of Tellanon.

The art of knot tying and getting out of jams, as mastered by Humbol, famed airman and adventurer.

Assorted other surprises.

Notes to self (and others):

1. *After Ea'ae's near destruction at the hands of the Cabal, I was tasked with compiling a knowledge reserve that could be strategically deployed should we ever face a similar incursion or threat again.*[2]

2. *The expertise so compiled has been included in this and like volumes and*

> *similar repositories intended for edification and improvement within various high Arts of Ea'ae.*[3]

3. *The knowledge and skills contained herein will not, however, be available for implantation and integration until after a complete bioassay and parapsychological assessment by the synthetic intelligence incorporated into this compendium.*[4]

4. *Only when you are deemed sufficiently prepared, responsible, and of appropriate mind will you be allowed to access desired knowledge.*[5]

5. *The information contained herein has been thoroughly encrypted, confusticated, and imbroglioed. Do not try to hack, decipher, or intercept this information without proper approval.*[6]

6. *You will not like what happens if you do.*[7]

7. *May this knowledge help you achieve the highest imaginings of the human spirit.*[8]

8. *And also keep your stomach full.*

9. *Assessment will begin upon selection of any desired topic.*

GLOSSARY OF TERMS
PEOPLE, PLACES, AND THINGS

Abyss – a general name often used for extradimensional regions home to daemonic creatures of Darkness and despair. Also called *nether realms*.

Adamantium – an exceedingly strong magical metal.

Aerie – a name commonly used for the peaks and summits claimed by dragons as their homes.

Aeromancy – the study of the air and its currents, the manipulation of its energies, and the fashioning of airships.

Aerya – literally, "Light" or "air." An Elven term for the living energy of the universe. The concept of *Aerya* encompasses all forms of magical energetic expression in a single totality from the universal source to the personal creation—both chi and Yuan-chi. See also *Yuan-chi* and *chi*.

Aerya Etherum – literally, "highest air" or "highest breath." Alternatively, "first breath" or "source of breath." An Elven term for the source of the *Aerya*: the formless, boundless Void, source of limitless potential. See also *Wuji*.

Age – any extensive period of time. Typically thought of as representing one thousand years, though events of particular significance may also define its limits.

Airship – magically powered ships in as many shapes as the mind can imagine found plying the air currents and trade routes throughout Ea'ae and beyond. See also *aeromancy*.

Alchemical – Paratechnological study revolving around understanding the higher chemistries of the macroverse's functioning. Just as physical laws govern natural phenomena, and metamagical laws govern magical occurrences, alchemical laws govern the interactions between the two.

Allomorph – a being capable of taking on various shapes and guises, potentially augmenting its own intrinsic abilities, while retaining its primary core awareness, sense of self, and intelligence. The *Jira S'al Alann* are one such example.

Antientropics – the study of creating energy and adding energy back to systems, devices, and entities.

Anubaraëthi – literally, "Spawn of the Shadow," or "Shadow made manifest." A general Elven name for greater, sentient daemons. Sometimes called *Dread Lords*.

Anubavaeri – literally, "Spawn of the Flame," or "Spawn of the Fire." An Elven name for powerful daemons of flame.

Anuvaerya – literally, "Children of the Light." An Elven name for those Elves who have willingly left the bounds of the body to explore the realms of the mind and spirit. The existence of *Anuvaerya* is a closely guarded secret, known only to a few Elf-friends outside the Elven people.

Anuvatali – literally, "Children of the Dawn," or "Children of the New Morn." An Elven name for the half-Elven children of Men and Elves born on Ea'ae.

Anuvatari – literally, "Children of the Sun." An Elven name for those Elves who first came to Ea'ae.

Anuvatari'aliana– literally, "of one voice with the Children of the Sun" or "friend-kin of the Children of the Sun." An Elven name for those people of any race taken in by the Elves and taught something of their ways, or those who are trusted and respected as Elf-kin.

Archfiend – a general name for a daemon, particularly in reference to powerful daemons that have usurped dominion over lesser representatives of their own kind.

Archlich – a particularly powerful lich, often a powerful deceased practitioner of magic. See *lich*.

Archmage – a highly accomplished or powerful magician.

Archmathematics – higher order mathematics, modeling, and cognitive frameworks used in Paratechnological studies.

ARMED – Allomorphic Recombinatorial Multidimensional Extravehicular Drones. A flexible, multi-faceted, shape-changing drone system invented by Spreesprocket. Also called *sentry drones*.

Art – a calling, particularly one magical in nature.

Baera – "Brendle the All-Father" in the tongue of the Dwarves.

Baera'Dur – literally, "Brendle's bulwark" in the tongue of the Dwarves. Called *Dreadnaughts* by Men.

Baeradun – a legendary Dwarven hero known to burst into flames. Sometimes called "Burning Beard".

Beyond – a general term for other dimensions in the multiverse, often in reference to the nether realms. See *Abyss*.

Biomimetics – an area of Paratechnological research focusing on the understanding of biological functions, their governing principles, improvement, and alteration.

Blade Master – a highly proficient teacher of hand-to-hand combat in the Home Guard.

Blade Singer – see *Caer'collas*.

Bor'Banna – literally, "bearded demon." A name for the Dwarven masters of the axe, imbued by the remnants of power from Brendle's fire.

Bot – short for robot, particularly with regard to Paratechnological clockwork devices made by Tinkerers that may or may not manifest synthetic intelligence capable of independent thought.

Brendle – The All-Father. Dwarven god of the forge and, in the eyes of the Dwarves, the creator of the known universe. Called *Baera* in the tongue of the Dwarves.

Brendle's Flame – see *Brendle's Spark*.

Brendle's Spark – the remaining embers from Brendle's original flame and forge when Brendle first wrought the universe under hammer, anvil, and flame. The remaining embers even now bring forth life and magic into the universe. Also, the fires at the heart of the *Daerdaana'Duin*, the *Bor'Banna's* highest known skill, where the exponent merges directly with Brendle's flames. Also called *Brendle's Flame*. An analogue to *Aerya* and Yuan-chi in Dwarven cosmology.

Brendle's Tears – the finest of Dwarven ales. Reputed to be so wondrous and flavorful that Brendle himself cries tears of joy and amazement with each sip.

The Cabal –A sinister alliance of dark mages, fallen Priests, extradimensional beings, and other creatures of might bent on not only domination but power. Known by many other names, including the Order of the Lidded Eye, the Fallen, the Light Fallen, the Order of the Burning Eye, and the Order of the Hooded Gaze. Called Liúxīng Làngrén by the Priests of K'un Lun. Often symbolized by a blazing sigil of a closed eye.

Caer'collas – a Q'sharian blade master. Often called *Blade Singers* by those who watch their masterful interplay of magic and blade work.

Champion of Light – a general honorific for those who have earned great esteem fighting the forces of Darkness. Also, a title for one of great accomplishment within the Dalaren Ka.

Chi – Qi; breath, air, or vapor of particular significance in Taoism and Eastern medicine. From a Taoist perspective, the chi is the vital energy or life force that enlivens and pervades all things. Chi gung—chi kung or qigong—are exercises to build and strengthen chi flow. Along with shen and ching, one of the Three Treasures essential to human life. Chi is a less subtle and refined form of the Yuan-chi, the universal potential. The fire that does not burn.

Clockwork – a general name for a particular branch or type of Paratechnology focusing on magically animated contraptions of any shape, size, and function, often resembling machines and robots but not limited to any specific shape. A particular specialty of Gnomish Paratechnological Tinkerers.

Common – see *Common Tongue*.

Common Tongue – a universal language used across Ea'ae to facilitate nonmagical communication. Also called *Common*.

Craft – higher magical skills. An umbrella term inclusive of various branches of magic including unique talents and abilities native to particular races, guilds, and tribes.

DADD – Dwarves Against Drunk Dragons. Also, Dragons Against Drunk Dwarves.

Daemon – a general name for extradimensional creatures with hostile intent or for those otherworldly creatures that feed and prey upon the energies of the living. Also called *infernals*.

Daerdaana'Duin – literally, "to become the heart of fire" or "to become the heart of the forge". One of the highest skills of the *Bor'Banna*, wherein the practitioner wreaths himself in the flames of Brendle's forge, becoming a direct manifestation of Brendle's power and one with its heat, energy, and vitality. In times of old, these warriors cloaked themselves in flames, striking down foes directly with Brendle's might. See *Brendle's Spark*.

Daer'Duin – literally, 'heart of fire' or 'heart of the forge'. Given Dwarven name for Slate Flintforge.

Dagron Grey Beard – a famous Dwarven *Dur'kazak* of old.

Darkness – a general term for those beings opposed to the Light and Life it engenders and who would subvert, pervert, or otherwise mar Its presence and manifestation. Also a general term for the corruption of the energy of life, the Light, itself.

Delving – a general name for any Dwarven city or outpost. See also *undermount*.

Deur Spricken Sprack – Gnomish for "the Omnispark." See also *Phlogiston* and *Omnispark*.

Djazoth Al'Zann – a world conquering antihero, cultivator of rare orchids, and collector of stuffed bunnies.

Doerdaana'Duin – literally, "the dance of the heart of fire" or "to dance in the heart of the forge". One form of Dwarven axe work known for its fluid strikes and counters, commonly used by particularly adept *Bor'Banna*.

Dragonflight – a group of dragons living and moving together.

Dragons – along with the *Aeryn D'al*, one of the oldest races of Ea'ae. Steeped in magic and power, dragons are feared by all who cross their path. As complex as they are storied, dragons are as diverse as their characters and can wield power rivaled only by the gods themselves.

Drake – dragon.

Dread Lord – a general name for higher-order, more powerful daemons granted intelligence and power far beyond their peers. Called *Anubaraëthi*, Children of the Shadow, by Elves.

Dreadnaught – a Dwarven warrior specializing in heavy combat. Utilizing enchanted, rune-etched full plate armor along with two-handed axes, hammers, and maces, Dreadnaughts earn their place at the fore of the battlefield by fighting against the most implacable foes. Famous as much for their rallying battle cries and songs—along with their fear-inducing chants and dirges—as for their blades. Called *Baera'Dur* in the tongue of Dwarves.

Drothman – a famous Dwarven hero.

Druids – protectors of the wilds, guardians of nature, and lovers of freedom. First students of the *Indural*.

Dunédâne – literally, "deep delver". Name for the Dwarves among their own kind and the Karadüm.

Duraeleon – "The Light Bringer", bane of Adrael the Black, ancient axe of Ithilieon. Wielded by Slate Flintforge.

Durden – literally, "valiant heart". A Dwarven rune that serves to protect against fear and indecision when properly enchanted.

Durin – a famous Dwarven hero from times of yore.

Dur'kazak – literally, "fire shaper." A Dwarven master smith skilled in the art and craft of metallurgy, elemental magics, and rune crafting known as *Karaduen*.

Dwarves – along with Elves, Gnomes, and Men, one of the four most prominent races on Ea'ae. Dwarves are short, hearty, and solidly built, and are known for their ability to work metal. They excel at reading the earth and mining. Their keen knowledge of metals and runes allows for the creation of powerful works of Craft. Also called *Dunédâne*.

Ea'ae – "The world." Home to magical creatures and races of many shapes, cultures, and forms. Also, an exceptional book series.

EGAD – see the *Every Gnome's Anti-Intelligence Device*.

Elf-kin – Those people of any race taken in by the Elves and taught something of their ways. Sometimes called Elf-friends or *Anuvatari'aliana* in the tongue of the Elves.

Elves – a fey race at home among the trees and dells of Ea'ae. Elves are a race of great Craft and knowledge that made peace with the land long before the coming of Men and Dwarves and many other sentient races. It is said that magic is the lifeblood of the Elves. Often called Lords of the Wood or Tree Singers by Men, although not all Elves are indeed *Iyela*. Those Elves on Ea'ae are the *Anuvatari*.

The Enemy – Ur'Daus, the Darkness between dimensions. Also known as the Creeping Shadow, Destroyer of Light, the Umbral Lord, the Devourer of Worlds, among many other names and curses.

ENNIS – see *Epistemic Noetic Numenetic Integrating Summator*.

Epistemic Noetic Numenetic Integrating Summator – a multifunctional Gnomish device with capabilities ranging from measurement and systematic evaluation of phenomena, data analysis, computation, and communication to independent reasoning, learning aid, thought transference, and toothbrush. Also called *ENNIS* for short.

Every Gnome's Anti-Intelligence Device – a Paratechnological defensive system, suitable for espionage, surveillance, and camouflage, added to items ranging in size from personal armor to airships. The Every Gnome's Anti-Intelligence Device replicates the surrounding environmental variables and superimposes them over the object protected by the defensive system, rendering it indistinguishable from its surroundings. Sometimes referred to as EGAD or, more specifically and to add to the general air of confusion and embellishment around Gnomish devices, as the Every Gnome's Anti-Intelligence Clandestine Apparatus version 3.1, Corvette Class.

Evility – the expression of the primacy of an individual's needs and interests before the needs and interests of the group or placing the needs of one society ahead of another. The opposite of civility.

Extrabiology – the extension and expansion of biological systems, processes, and representations.

Face of the Mountain – a Dwarven term for an unreadable, stoic visage, as unchanging and unyielding as the mountain rock, particularly suited for floundering and confounding others.

Festival of the Clans – a large gathering of Dwarven clans filled with celebrations, competitions, reunions, feasting, drinking, sharing of lore, addressing of grievances, and forging of alliances.

Fiersayne – the brood and broodmates of Cersaegian.

Flashwhistle Boomblaster – A Gnomish Paratechnologist known for his particularly explosive zest for discovery and knack with incendiary devices.

Fria al'Othra – literally, "eyes of true vision." An Elven term for the universal perspective of the *Iyela*.

Früea – a Dwarven master artisan. The skills of a *Früea* range from creating fine jewelry and ornamentation to complex magical and mechanical artifices.

FTP – faster than physics. Gnomish Paratechnological communications system that allows communications faster than allowed by the (Non)Standard Model of physics.

Future history – the Paratechnological study of outcomes and possibilities.

GastroGnome – Gnomish lover of fine foods.

Gnomes – a race of short stature but of broad mind known for their creativity, imagination, and Paratechnological aptitude. Originators of Paratechnology, famed Tinkerers, often unable to leave well enough alone. Distant relatives of Dwarves.

Gnomeproof – a Dwarven colloquialism for foolproof.

Gnomosphere – Gnomish term for the noosphere.

GPE – Gnomish Protective Equipment.

Günda – literally, "Dwarf excrement." An Orcish curse.

Henosis – a theurgical practice whose ultimate aim is unification with and expression of the Divine Light.

Homeworld – planet of origin or primary habitation for a race, species, or group.

Hröthe – literally, "divine healing". A Dwarven *Karaduen* offering a one-time boon of healing from a grievous or debilitating wound.

Human – see *humanity*. A general name for an individual member of any of the sentient races on Ea'ae.

Humanity – a general name for all humanoid races on Ea'ae. Men, Dwarves, Gnomes, *Indural,* and other sentient races of Ea'ae are included under this broad description. As a naturalized race, Elves, too, are considered part of Humanity, although they are genetically distinct from the other humanoid races.

Hürn – literally, "evil's bane". A Dwarven rune used for protection from evil.

Idealized engineering – the practical translation of Paratechnological ideas to actuality.

Illdrassil – literally, "Spire of the Heavens" or "Tree of Heaven" in the Old Tongue of Men. The home of the Council, Tellanon's ruling body and the Home Guard. A vast repository of magical energies that empowers the city in the sky.

Indural – one trained in the magic, lore, and woodcraft of the forest giants.

Infernal – a daemon.

Iyela – an Elven lorekeeper, wonder worker, tree singer, and shaper.

Known for their ability to commune with the spirit of trees and request the boon of their heartwood, the *Aeryn Sh'al*. Called Tree Singers by Men.

Jira S'al Alann – literally, "People of the Imagining". A race of changelings able to shift their guise and abilities depending upon their magical development and attunement. See also *allomorph*.

Karaduen – a Dwarven word meaning "Light's ward" or "Light's seal." Special Dwarven runes and symbols often employed by *Dur'Kazak* and *Kor'-Dannan* in the crafting of artifacts and the creation of spells and enchantments.

Kazzak – literally, "marks of honor" in the tongue of the Dwarves. Symbols, tokens, and items of repute woven into a *Bor'Banna*'s beard as badges of honor and accomplishment. Also common among other Dwarves.

Khuerkanna – a famous Dwarven general known for his triumphant last stand against the Orcs and their allies in the Battle of the Broken Blade.

Kiloboulder – a Gnomish unit of force, energy output, and weight.

Koerdian Cave Bear – a species of gigantic cave bear particularly respected by Dwarves for their strength, perseverance, and indomitable spirit.

Kor'Dannan – Dwarven Priests of Brendle given the keeping and wisdom of his fires, Brendle's Spark. Fierce warriors equally adept at healing and providing succor.

Lich – undead beings sustained by twisted magical energies.

Life – all living beings taken as a whole.

The Light – the ambient energy of the universe; the energy of Life enlivening all of existence. Considered holy, sacred, and heavenly. See also *Aerya*, *chi*, ching, dalare, *Deur Spricken Sprack*, *Omnispark*, *Phlogiston*, shen, *Brendle's Spark*, and *Yuan-chi*.

Loess – literally, "Heaven's shielding". A protective Dwarven rune meant for use against supernatural forces.

Ludaceous Vaer Mordicanum – wondrous scribe, scholar, and luminary. One of the greatest intellects of his or any generation.[1]

Mulogo's note:

1. *Or so he thinks.*

Luerdan – literally, "troll dung" in the tongue of the Dwarves.

Macrocosmos – see *macroverse*.

Macroverse – the totality of multi-dimensional existence, inclusive of all planes, alternate universes, and extradimensional regions. See *multiverse*. Also megacosm or macrocosmos.

Magic – the translation of the possible into the actual, the imagined into the real. The three primary components of magical practice are often understood as: *belief*, faith that an individual can take an active part in universal creation; *intent* (or will), the shaping of this belief to guide in creation; and *imagination*, the vision or desired outcome made possible by belief and shaped by intent.

The wellspring of magic is universal energy. Depending upon the tradition, this source is known as Yuan-chi, Brendle's Spark, Phlogiston and the Omnispark, *Aerya*, and Light, among others. This universal energy is often understood as the source and fuel of life, the chi. Sometimes broken into greater and lesser magics referencing the differentiation between the universal source energy—Yuan-chi, Phlogiston, *Aerya*, Light, and celestial or divine magics—and the intrinsic ambient energies of life: the chi.

See also *Yuan-chi, chi, Brendle's Spark, Phlogiston* and *Omnispark, Aerya,* and *the Light*.

Major and Minor Shielding – a complex combination of spells serving to protect the recipient from arcane damage and hostile spells (the Major Shield); while also guarding against physical damage, impacts, blows, cuts, and the like (the Minor Shield).

Mauguer – a Dwarven brewmaster. Of their many secret arts, brewing Brendle's Tears is the most closely guarded.

Megacosm – see *multiverse* or *macroverse*.

Men – the youngest and most prolific race of Ea'ae. Native flexibility and intuitiveness allows Men to excel in many fields, progressing quickly through their chosen arts.

Metamagics – the study of magic in and of itself, its laws, and governing principles.

Mithril – a particularly light, yet strong, magical metal.

Möerak – a skilled Dwarven miner with an uncanny ability to uncover valuable veins of ore, minerals, and gems.

Mulogo – accomplished wizard known for many magical theories and refinements as well as drafting *Mulogo's Treatise on Wizardry*.[2]

Scribe's note:

1. *A* cynical old curmudgeon who fancies himself something of a wizard.

Multimodal computational panlogic – the theory of structured and unstructured reasoning, rational and irrational decision-making, and generally making things up.

Multiverse – the entirety of multidimensional space, inclusive of alternate universes, planes, and dimensions. Also macroverse and megacosm.

Mysteries – a general name for types or classes of magic.

Nether realms – extradimensional planes home to infernals and other fiendish creatures. See *Abyss*.

New Unified Mental-Energetic Noesis – NUMEN. A synthetic Paratechnological being of great mental and physical capacity, able to take on many shapes, forms, and functions. An extension of the Paratechnology developed in the TAMERS units without need of an operator, as the NUMEN is guided by its own intelligence. Also, a play on words among Paratechnologists for their magical-technological creations that may one day supersede them.

Noeldri – literally, "flowing water". A Dwarven rune granting grace and agility both physically and mentally.

Noerlag[3] – a double-bladed great axe of high renown. Chosen weapon of Urdaen Doomhammer. Called *Fellblade* by the Dwarves. Called *Spinetickler* by the Orcs. Composer of texts of Dwarven lore. Of absolutely and most assuredly no relation to Duraeleon.

Dwarf's Note:

1. *A lyin' cur with a tongue as sharp as its treacherous blade.*

Noosphere – the realm of the mind, the collective consciousness, or the sphere of thought. A general name for the metamagical plane allowing for the shared existence and interaction both within and between various synthetic intelligences. A Paratechnological creation of the highest order. Also references the sphere of thought, mind, or knowledge itself. Also called the *Gnomosphere*.

Notional physics – the Paratechnological study of the higher (and lower) laws of the universe, the greater macroverse, and its various subsets.

Nüaerblun – literally, "dragon dung" in the tongue of the Dwarves. Often used as a Dwarven insult.

Nüaer'Daer – literally, "life's heart." A Dwarven term for dragons.

Nüaer'Duin – literally, "dragon fire" or "life's fire" in the tongue of the Dwarves. Among the Dwarves, dragon fire is respected for its magical properties and power so like the heat of Brendle's forge.

NUMEN – see *New Unified Mental-Energetic Noesis.*

Occlusion – a Paratechnologist known for his overzealous shaving habits.

Occlusion's razor – a simple axiom arrived at by Occlusion after much trial, error, and many, many cuts… getting the most for the least.

Oedenara – literally, "daemon's heart." A crystalline gem, found at the heart of some daemons, that has powerful magical properties and is of much practical use.

Omnicron – a Paratechnological device capable of generating and sustaining immersive, non-virtual actualities.

Omnispark – Gnomish conception of the ignited or expressed source of life unending, ever-changing and evolving, fueled by Phlogiston. *Deur Spricken Sprack* in Gnomish. Also called Yuan-chi, *magic, Aerya, Brendle's Spark,* and *the Light,* among other terms, by other races.

Orcs – a large and prolific evil race spread through the wilds and caverns of Ea'ae. Orcs are strong, aggressive, and full of guile, a race of warriors and shaman. Working in league with Trolls and Ogres, Orcs often lead their slower witted brethren on the field of battle.

Paladin – a holy warrior dedicated to and empowered by the Light. Paladins are vanquishers of evil, banishers of the unholy, adjudicators and arbiters, healers and almsmen. Many variants exist, some dedicated to particular deities and powerful entities, each with different talents, specialties, and ethos. The Dalaren Ka are one such group.

Parapsychology – the magical study of the mind, its features, moods, states, and manifestations.

Paratechnology – literally, "beyond technology." The study of making the imagined real and actualizing the impossible. The art and science of applied magic and magical technologies. Paratechnological apprehension is shared across many races, however the Gnomes' natural curiosity and creativity have brought Paratechnological expertise to its current refined state and have helped to spread its knowledge throughout the cosmos.

Phlogiston – called *Deur Spricken Sprack* in the tongue of Gnomes. In Gnomish reckoning, the invisible spark of life pervading the universe akin to an invisible metastate of gaseous energetic conductance. Once ignited, Phlogiston fuels all life as the Omnispark. When manipulated by will, the Phlogiston gives rise to magic. Also called Yuan-chi, *magic, Aerya, Brendle's Spark,* and *the Light,* among other terms, by other races and traditions.

Phylactery – an amulet, charm, or safeguard against harm or danger. Also, a vessel for relics.

Plane – one of many distinct layers of existence in the larger macro or multiverse. Often synonymous with universe or dimension.

Pocket dimension – a miniature space or reality created expressly for a specific purpose. In the case of the myriad pocket dimensions of Tellanon, these represent miniature universes intimately connected to Tellanon itself, extending its breadth and depth. More often, pocket dimensions are used to extend space within a given region—for example, to make the space within a bag or room larger.

Pocket fairy – small, often cantankerous fairies given to taking up residence in Gnomish pockets.

Powers – beings of great might, often extradimensional in origin.

Priest – one who has been accepted fully into the Order of the K'un Lun. See *Priest of K'un Lun.*

Priest of K'un Lun – an Order of mystics dedicated to the practice of various esoteric and martial traditions found nowhere else on Ea'ae. The way of the Priest is geared toward continual transformation and development within and without through the evolving practice of internal alchemy.

Priest of Maeth Onai – an order of magicians from the cold Northlands that practices a unique blend of mundane and divine magics whereby divine energies are channeled to perform traditional and inimitable spells.

Projection – a general term for a multi-dimensional representation of an object, such as a magical hologram or depiction. Also a reference to life-like, immersive news feeds displaying current happenings and items of worth.

Psion – a being gifted mentally and psychically.

Psionics – psychic mental powers and abilities as expressed by a psion.

Rakshasha – Sanskrit for demon. A race of powerful feline daemonic sorcerers in league with the Cabal.

Saedeus Moerdencanum – warlock, dictator, despot, and all-around not so nice guy. Saedeus's empire spread far and wide across several galaxies and planes through a pernicious combination of fell necromantic sorceries and high technologies. Saedeus's reign of intergalactic terror was ended when his conquests disrupted the vegetable supply of a particularly enterprising group of Gnomes with an inordinate fondness for rutabagas.

SAVERS – see *Self Actuated Variable Emergency Response System*.

Sceaduwulf – literally, "shadow wolf." A spectral wolf.

Schema – The patterning, diagramming, representation, and planning of Paratechnological devices, theorems, strategies, and abstractions.

Scierdyas – literally, "spectral dragons." Energetic beings very similar in appearance to dragons summoned from the unholy nether realms of the darkest abysms.

Self-Actuated Variable Emergency Response System – a Paratechnological clockwork emergency response bot of Gnomish invention, capable of independently responding to, assessing, and reacting to multiple life-threatening situations. Called *SAVERS* for short.

Sentry drones – a general name for Paratechnological defensive drones. See also *ARMED*.

Shade – a nebulous creature of Darkness.

Shadow – a general term for creatures of Darkness and their ilk. Those opposed to the energy of Life in all its manifestations and who seek to subvert, pervert, consume, or otherwise destroy the Light in all its manifold expressions.

Shadowkin – a general term for creatures of Darkness. See *Shadow*.

Shaur'Daus – literally, a "Stalker of Darkness" in the tongue of the Dracodaerans. Draconic warriors wreathed in the fires of heaven that do battle against the creatures of Darkness across the cosmos and beyond.

Shen Po – master of the void palm, one of the fallen founding fathers of the K'un Lun, member of the Cabal, and one time teacher of Master Wei.

Shiny – a highly sought after, much admired quality in Paratechnology. Shiny is a very complex term with many shades of meaning. Except when its meaning is simple. Typically understood as desirable or bright and highly reflective; or the state of being such. Discussions of shiny are never dull.

Skael – a people of nomadic traders who travel the skies in airships plying their wares.

Spreesprocket Goldpulley – Gnomish Paratechnologist and humble writer of many insightful texts.

Südaer – a Dwarven lorekeeper and magician.

Super sack – a magical Gnomish bottomless bag. Super sacks are often cluttered, disorganized, and very difficult to retrieve items from, especially within a short, highly critical period of time.

Suprachemistry – the study of how magical and nonmagical systems, compounds, elements, entities, and components interact, react, behave, change, and develop.

Synthetic intelligence – a Paratechnological term for the sentience resulting from the merger of two different intelligences. Typically, one intelligence is natural and the other is artificial, one is organic and the other is disembodied or a metamagical complex arising from technical sophistication, or one intelligence is formed explicitly to merge with and augment another. Far different from the Abstract and Construct's relationship with Citizens, for example, wherein one intelligence serves another directly and indirectly, synthetic intelligences are the result of a complete union between two disparate awarenesses, the resulting union having complete access to the knowledge and capabilities of both. Most typically, one intelligence is created explicitly to merge with and augment another, extending the field of sentient consciousness into directions and dimensions limited only by the imagination.

Also a reference to any created intelligence.

Taerris'thule – literally, "old home." Formerly a religious city and home to the seal of Eldre'gheu. Sometimes referred to as the City of the Fallen Gods.

TAMERS – see *Transmorphic Actionable Multidimensional Exo-Robotic System*.

Tellanon – literally, "Heaven's Landing" in the Old Tongue of Men. A spectacular floating island city in the sky, a center of commerce and diplomacy, and a starting point for both interstellar and interdimensional travel. Home of Illdrassil, the Home Guard, and Paratechnologists on Ea'ae.

Thane – traditional leader of a Dwarven clan.

Tinkerers – Paratechnologists focusing on clockwork devices melding magic and technology in forms often resembling complex mechanical devices. Most often associated with Gnomish Paratechnologists due to their strong imaginative mechanical tendencies.

Transmorphic Actionable Multidimensional Exo-Robotic System – A multi-functional, transforming exoarmor system created by Spreesprocket. Also known as TAMERS.

Traveling – teleportation or any other form of instantaneous travel ,whether inter- or intra-dimensional.

The Umbral Lord – see *the Enemy* or *Ur'Daus*.

Undermount – a general name for any Dwarven city or a Dwarven occupied region. Typically located in the bedrock beneath mountains. Undermounts are composed of Dwarven fastnesses and attendant halls and byways that grow within the roots of the hills. Also called delvings, though delvings are typically smaller in scale.

Ungar – literally, "earthen might". A Dwarven rune granting physical strength and endurance.

Urdaea – Urdaen's granddaughter.

Urdaen "Flamebeard" Doomhammer – Dwarven hero and inspiration for many a tome and tale. Most fortunate wielder of Noerlag.

Ur'Daena – literally, "the axe's lament." The uniquely Dwarven art of the axe. Many styles and forms are known, each generally ascribed to a specific family, clan, or thanedom. Variations in styles—from the use of great two-handed war axes taller than a man suited to the openness of the battlefield, to forms of double-bladed combat better suited to the close quarters of a mineshaft—are all practiced with distinctly Dwarven fervor.

When practiced by a master, a *Bor'Banna*, these styles rely as much on channeling the remnants of Brendle's original creation magic through the axe as they do on physical prowess for their efficacy. When wielded by a true master, the axe of the *Bor'Banna* is said to glow with the light and heat of Brendle's original forge.

Ur'Daus – literally, "The Darkness." Also known as the Enemy, the Creeping Shadow, the Devourer of Worlds, the Umbral Lord, the Great Devourer, and many others. A fathomless Light consuming Darkness trapped between dimensions in Ages long past.

Vanduen – literally, "divine regeneration". A Dwarven *Karaduen* that enhances healing capacities, speeding recovery and repair from exhaustion and injury.

Vöer – troll, in the tongue of the Dwarves.

Vöerdan – literally, "Troll saliva or spittle." A Dwarven insult.

Void – the wellspring of creation. The limitless potential underlying all existence.

Vradek – Orcish gruel made from ground bones simmered in blood.

Vyaera – literally, "wanderers along the path." An Elven term for those sharing the same path, quest, purpose, or journey.

War of Shadows – one name for the first war with the Cabal and their dark allies, waged on Ea'ae in the distant past.

Worgs – massive wolves used by Orcs as mounts in lieu of horses.

Wyrm – an ancient or powerful dragon.

Yerens – a noble race of yeti-like creatures. Singers of the worldsong. Called the Shapers of the True Song, Shapers, and Singers.

Younglings – a common name for Dwarven children.

Yuan-chi – the primordial energy, the inherent unrealized potential, of the universe; the celestial or divine *chi*.

HELP SPREAD THE WORD!

As an independent author, I live by your kind words, your enthusiasm, and your passion for good stories.

Whether these words transported you to another place, one you enjoyed wholeheartedly, or pushed you away without lasting impression, I would welcome your review of my book.

If you truly appreciated this book, spread the word to your friends, family, and random acquaintances. I would also love for you to visit me at either my website at www.josephjbailey.com or on my Facebook Author's Page.

If you would like to learn about future book releases, please consider signing up for my book announcement newsletter.

Many thanks and happy reading!

Joseph J. Bailey

ABOUT THE AUTHOR

Joe holds an advanced degree in environmental management from Duke University where he also studied religion with a focus on meditative, experiential, and transformative traditions. Additionally, he graduated with (dubious) honors from the Tellanon Institute of Noetic Knowledge, Education, and Research (TINKER), but has yet to put this knowledge to good use.

When not at play with his family, he enjoys reading, writing, and relaxation. When he can, Joe also practices various martial arts in which he has attained the Victim level of proficiency.

Joe is the author of over thirty fiction and nonfiction books and is a named inventor on multiple patents.

BY JOSEPH J. BAILEY

The Chronicles of the Fists trilogy:
    Shadow's Rise
    Shadow's Descent
    Lords of Light

The *Legacy of the Blade* trilogy:
    Soul Stealer
    Wild Mage
    Stone Singer

The *Orc PI* series:
    Grak – Private Instigator
    Grak – Orc on Vacation
    Grak – Gnomercy

The *Exceptional Advice for Adventurer Everywhere* series:
    Mulogo's Treatise on Wizardry

Everygnome's Guide to Paratechnology
Nemesis – A Good Guide for Bad Guys
Confessions of an Angry Dwarf

The *Spellslinger Chronicles* series:
    Infernal Fire
    Guns' Ghosts
    Spellslinger

Other works:
    Contagion
    Octopocalypse
    Out of the Box
    Zombies Forever
    Master of the Flying Broom - Sword Saint in Training
    Demon Hunter - The Misadventures of a Fallen Holy Knight

Joe is also working on something else but really cannot say more on the matter at present.

ACKNOWLEDGMENTS

I would like to thank my wife for her love and support; my beta readers for their willingness to enter worlds unlike any other; my friends for listening to my all-too-frequent updates and ideas; David Gatewood, my editor, for helping polish my vision; and all the readers who took a chance in reading my work.